TESTING TIMES FOR TABITHA BAIRD

Arabella Weir is an actress, comedian and writer best known for *The Fast Show*. She makes regular appearances on TV and radio and is a frequent contributor to national newspapers. She has written several books for adults including the international bestseller, *Does My Bum Look Big in This?*, and the Tabitha trilogy for younger readers. She lives in north London with her two teenagers and maybe a dog . . . soon.

The TABITHA trilogy

The Rise and Rise of Tabitha Baird
The Endless Trials of Tabitha Baird
Testing Times for Tabitha Baird

TESTING TIMES FOR TABITHA BAIRD

ARABELLA WEIR

Piccadilly
PRESS

First published in Great Britain in 2015
by Piccadilly Press
Northburgh House, 10 Northburgh Street,
London EC1V 0AT

www.piccadillypress.co.uk

A CIP catalogue record for this book
is available from the British Library.

ISBN: 978-1-848-12465-3

1 3 5 7 9 10 8 6 4 2

Typeset by Palimpsest Book Production Limited,
Falkirk, Stirlingshire
Printed and bound by Clays Ltd, St Ives Plc

Piccadilly Press is part of the Bonnier Publishing Group
www.bonnierpublishing.com

For my endlessly supportive co-parents,
Helen Castor and Jane Morgan,
my middle-aged, teenage pals

SPRING TERM WEEK 8

MONDAY

Loooooooook, I KNOW! I know I haven't written anything for absolutely aaaaaages. I know, I know, I know and I'm reeeeeeally, reeeeeally sorry — truly, deeply, madly sorry, promise. And I do feel bad about it. Honestly, I do, cross my heart. I should have written something, anything, even a few words. I know. I just sort of forgot and then once I'd forgotten I sort of got out of the habit and anyway I couldn't find you, my lovely notebook, for a while either. My pathetic loser of a little brother probably hid you to annoy me. But anyhoo, I'm back now and I PROMISE I will write a lot, all the time, every single day if I can, okay? BTW , though, don't worry, it's not like I haven't written anything for centuries because my life suddenly became soooo interesting and action-packed. I wish! Oh man (yes, 'oh man' is still A Cool Thing To Say, so obvs being Super Cool I still say it!), wouldn't that be THE BEST? As in — my life is so crazy busy I have no time to write — 'Can't write now, my private jet's about to take off driven by Hottie Pilot. All my bezzies are already on board and we're flying off to a boiling hot luxury desert island where there are no schools and no homework.' Hah, hah. AS IF. But wouldn't that just be sooooo fab? In fact, I'll bet anyone who really does have that sort of life doesn't ever even have time to write a diary or even a note. Not like me, then! I do have the time but, the truth is, I haven't had time for a bit, okay, all right, a bit too long. Anyway, I'm back now, so it's all okay, and I'll try to write every day . . . PROMISE.

Anyhoo — so, a quick catch-up . . . just to let you know what's been happening in the so-called centuries, hah, hah, that have passed when I didn't write anything . . . Erm . . . let me think . . . nothing exactly major has happened . . . Oh yeah, I've remembered, one pretty major thing has happened – Mum has FINALLY started giving me pocket money! Which is really great. It's only £4 a week, which, get this, Mum, of course, thinks is a fortune. Can you believe that? A fortune. Oh yeah, typical of Mum, my allowance came with a long, boring lecture about her only agreeing to it so that I could learn how to, her words, budget according to my needs! Hello?! Budget according to my needs?! What on earth is that supposed to mean?! I had absolutely no clue what she was talking about except that it seemed to me to be a pretty long speech to make about four pounds! And, get this, out of my oh-so-huge luxury allowance of £4 a week I am supposed to pay for any stuff I want (but 'obviously don't need' according to Mum, annoying or what?!), top up my own travel card (I only agreed to that because I walk to school and buses are free, so, you know, not a real biggie) and, wait for it, buy all my mates' birthday presents! I know, completely ridic or what?! I was really cross about that last bit.

I mean, like you can get any sort of decent present for £4. AS IF. And then Mum explained that she expected me to save up some of the £4 when I knew there was a birthday coming so that I could pay for it out of a few weeks' worth of money. Which, you know, is obvs another completely stupid idea of hers. I can barely be expected to survive on £4 a week, never mind less if I have to save money out of it. Totes ridic. Typical Mum said that she wasn't going to budge on that point and that that's what 'budget according to your means' means. (I looked it up afterwards, and it does actually mean making plans for the money you've got. Huh, I don't know why Mum thinks I need to learn to do that. Any idiot knows how to spend the money they've got. Derr.) Mum would not listen to me, even when I told her that everyone would hate me if I gave them crappy presents because I didn't have enough money to buy really nice ones because my mum was too tight to give me more. God, she can be so mean sometimes.

Anyway, it's really cool to have my own money now – it feels so grown up. I love it. Emz and Grace have also got pocket money but A'isha's dad is dragging his feet about giving it to her. He says it will make her too 'Western'! A'isha told us and then she laughed and said, 'So it's too Western to have pocket money but it's okay for me to go to school with boys. That's your Messed-up Muslim thinking again.'

So, now, when we all meet up to walk to school we go into the shop and buy chewing gum and magazines and stuff. I mean, I know we did that before sometimes but it was always with a £1 or £2 coin our mums had given us and expected (hilar) change from! Now it's our own money and we keep the change and can buy whatever we like . . . It's just so . . . I don't know . . . mature. Yeah, that's it, using your own money to buy your own things that no one's told you to get, you're deciding for yourself that you want it and then buy it without having to ask any grown-up if it's all right, and it feels mature and, like, sort of a bit sophisticated, you know?

So, what else is new? Well, it's not exactly new because it does happen every year, hah, hah, but it's my birthday in a couple of weeks – 25 March, to be precise. Isn't that the worst date of the whole entire year for a birthday?! Just my luck. It's not proper spring by then and it's hardly ever warm, so it's not like you can organise a picnic or anything outside-y. It's still practically winter and usually, almost always, raining or at least crummy weather on that day. But it's also not proper winter, like wintery and snowy, when you could organise a whole hot-chocolate-melting-marshmallows type of party either. I've always hated my birthday being on that date. I wish it were in June or July (defs not late July or August, though. They're the worst birthdays, when you're not at school and no one's around. The pits.) Anyway, don't suppose there's anything I can do now about changing the day I was born! So, I am going to be fourteen – and that is major! I don't know why but fourteen feels sooooo old. I looked up what you can do when you're fourteen and there's much more stuff you can do than when you're thirteen and the best ones are: I can get a part-time job ON A SCHOOLDAY and I can go into a bar and order a soft drink (how cool is that?!), and there was one completely random one, which was 'It is considered your own responsibility to wear a seat belt'. Yeah, right, like on the day you turn fourteen all of a sudden your parents are going to stop checking if you're wearing your seat belt and whizz off up the road at a hundred miles an hour with you rattling around in the back!? Anyway, we don't have a car so no 'being responsible for wearing a seat belt' for me! I'd love to get a job, though, that would be the coolest thing in the whole entire world.

So, I think . . . I've only just started thinking about this but I *think* I might have a party for my birthday

. . . I feel super nervous about it because obvs it would have to be here. I asked Mum if we could hire a hall or something and she just laughed — nice. Later, though, Gran and Mum said if I wanted to have a small party here then I could. I know it's really kind of Gran and everything but this house is so small and not trendy and I don't want my mates to think it's all a bit . . . I don't know . . . not amazingly fantastic.

IF, and it's only if now (I've got a bit of time to decide), I have a party I wonder what it should be . . . you know, what theme. Not fancy dress obvs. I'm way too old for that sort of thing. But maybe like . . . I don't know, people off the telly or pop stars, something like that? That's not fancy dress, is it? Mum did actually make a pretty good suggestion, amazingly, which was a 'mocktail' party — you know, it's like a cocktail party with loads of different, really fun cocktails, but without alcohol in them obviously. Gran loved that idea. 'Ooh, you could all dress up in cocktail dresses, like we all did in the sixties. You'd look gorgeous,' she sort of squealed when Mum mentioned it. That would be quite a laugh. Don't know about looking gorgeous,

I don't ever feel exactly gorgeous, but it was sweet of Gran to say it. I might do that but I don't want to look like I'm making too much of a super big deal out of it, though. You know, like I'm trying really hard to have an amazing party. I'm worried it'll make me look desperate.

Hmm . . . is that a bit . . . I don't know . . . silly? Or is not trying really hard how you stay the coolest kid at school? Because, you know, if you think about it no one who tries really hard at anything, especially not at school, is ever considered super cool, but then, on the other hand, if you love doing something, not trying your best at it is just stupid. Completely ridic in fact.

For example, and this is top secret, not even my bezzies have worked it out yet, I really love ESC now (that's what they call religious education at HAC). It's not because I've gone all religious-y but because, as Ms Cantor (you know, the one we're allowed to call by her first name, Eve, if the head's not around) says, these days learning about religion is really more about learning about other cultures and 'engaging in healthy argument' about the rules and regulations of cultures different from yours. And, guess what, I've discovered that I am really good at arguing. Hah, hah. *Quelle surprise!* (That's French for 'what a surprise'. Good, isn't it?!) But what I love in ESC is not arguing like I do with that nerdy knicks Luke, my totally mankenstein, majorly yuck little brother – it's . . . wait for it . . . 'constructive debate' Miss calls it. What that means, according to Miss, is that you can disagree with what someone else says or believes in, you just can't insult it or say they're wrong. You have to find ways of arguing against their way of life or beliefs, whatever, but properly. You know, not saying 'That's stupid or wrong or pathetic'. And, it turns out, I AM SO GOOD AT IT! That's probably why I love it! Hah, hah. I'm not being a big head, though. Miss is the one who said that. It's probably all the practice I got from years of arguing with Luke.

So, you see, that's something I'm actually good at and like being good at but don't really want everyone to know about. Does that make sense? I don't think that means I'm turning into a swot – AS IF – but it does mean I pay more attention in that class because I want to be involved. Hmm, it's tricky, isn't it? It's quite a big deal, you know — well, for me it is — how to be good at an actual school subject AND also stay coolest in my year?!

Also, we've got to choose our GCSE options in a couple of weeks, which is SUPER MAJOR. I have absolutely no clue what I'm going to pick. So wish there was a GCSE in arguing. I'd defs get an A* in that!

SPRING TERM
WEEK 9

MOST EMBARRASSING
THING EVER

Don't think I said — Mum is still going out with Dumbledore Chops. Yuck. You will never believe this but the other day she actually said with a big smile on her face, 'I guess Frank is now officially my boyfriend,' and then she did a little laugh. Bleurgh. Mankenstein or what? How extra is that? 'Officially my boyfriend'?! Oh, please, and anyway, so what? And like we all needed a big announcement. It's pretty obvious — pass the sick bag — as he's round here all the time and when he's not they're always going out to do stuff together. So, like, derr, I didn't think he was her bezzie or workmate or anything. Anyway, Mum doesn't have workmates because she writes her column from home, so she's Nelly No Mates as far as that goes. Oh look, I'm not being mean about Mum. Her blog, now column, is, she says, going really well and gets lots of 'traffic' (hello, traffic in a newspaper?!) and, apparently, 'It's all about traffic, darling'. Hah, you're telling me, when you're stuck on a bus for ages it is defs all about traffic! But I don't think Mum means that same kind of traffic.

And yeah, get this, Luke, the most annoying brother in the world, isn't going to come to HAC this September. He's going to some boys-only school (I know, extra or what?!) that he had to do an exam to get into and it's not around here either. He's got to travel nearly an hour to get there. Because of him supposedly being so brainy, in other words a Super Nerd, Mum decided he should try this school's Brainboxes-Only exam and he passed. Bully for him.

I'm sort of relieved he's not coming to HAC because as much as I hate his guts I know I'd have ended up looking out for him. Of course I would. He is my little brother, even if he is The Most Annoying Know-It-All in the Entire World. But also I do feel a bit funny that he's going to some not-for-ordinary-kids school. It feels a bit like he's more special than me in a way, like he's better than me. Mum is thrilled to bits that he's got in and I distinctly remember that she couldn't care less where I went when we moved to London. Well, that's not exactly true. HAC is where she went, a trillion years ago, but she never once suggested I try for a school where you have to do an exam or anything like that. Obviously she couldn't think about another private school, like the place I was at before Mum and Dad split up, because she doesn't have the money any more but, still, she defs didn't once mention anywhere except HAC.

I do love it at HAC, though, and I don't want to be anywhere else and I've got my totes couldn't-live-without-them bezzies — Emz, A'isha and Grace — but it would be nice if my own mother weren't so completely obvious all the time about preferring Luke to me.

But at least, thank god, Luke is on my side about Dumbledore Chops. We both think he is yucky, way too old for Mum — he's at least ten years older than her — and just sort of generally annoying, particularly with the way he nods his head while you're talking and says 'yeah, yeah, yeah' at the same time, and his all-over totes embarrassing way of trying to be down with the kids. When Luke and I make faces about him, after he's been here, Gran always says things like 'You should be happy for your mother' and 'It's nice for your mum to have a companion'. Maybe, but not him! If Mum absolutely must go out with someone why can't it be someone much younger and more cool and hip? Dumbledore Chops is so old he is actually retired. Retired, as in *so old he's stopped working*. How extra is that?! Mum is going out with a Retired Man! I mean, come on, hellooooo? She might as well be going out with an old-age pensioner. Oh god, I suppose he IS, officially, like, you know, an actual old-age pensioner. Great. My mum is going out with an OAP. I know Gran is an OAP but she's supposed to be; she's a granny. Unless your mum had you when she was really super young, like practically-only-just-left-school young then all grannies are OAPs! But your own mother's boyfriend collecting his pension?! Could anything in the whole world be less cool? Just kill me now. I will admit one good thing about Dumbledore Chops, I suppose, is that he is more of a Proper Grown-Up than Dad is – you know, has had a job, owns his own place, probably has savings, all that sort of Grown-Up Stuff. BUT he is nowhere near as handsome or fun or funny as Dad. How can Mum prefer him?

DUMBLEDORE CHOPS
← NOT A COOL BEARD

If Mum marries Dumbledore Chops I am going to refuse to live with them. And that is that. And I'm pretty sure Luke will too. I am not going to live with him whatever happens. Ever. If Mum thinks he's so marvellous and wonderful she can live with him but I'll stay with Gran. Anyway, Mum can't marry him because she's still married to Dad, well, at least, I think she is. She's never mentioned getting divorced. It's weird, actually, because, secretly — literally not one other person in the world knows this — I sort of like it that Mum and Dad are still married. It feels like it means there's still a bit of hope that they might get back together.

I'm probably being babyish hoping for that. I mean, there are no actual signs that they might get back together as far as I know. When Luke and I speak to Dad it's always on our mobiles — if we didn't have them he'd have to ring the house phone and then he might accidentally get Mum and then if they talked they might realise they missed each other . . . Oh, I really wish they hadn't split up. I don't like having to think about these horrible sad things. I guess I know deep down it's all silly fantasy stuff that they'll get back together. I think I sort of understand why they had to break up. I know Dad's hopeless and can't stop drinking. I'm not saying it's Mum's fault. I know it isn't. But she must have known what he was like way back, even before she had Luke and me. Mum said to me once: 'An addict's only real love is his addiction and no matter how much you love someone you can't compete with that.' She wasn't being horrible about Dad. She said it in a quite matter-of-fact-y voice, like she was giving me some information. I did wonder if she was sort of saying she still loved him but that it was a waste of time. I can't bear to think of Mum still loving Dad but giving up.

I hate thinking about this stuff, just hate it. I wish they'd stayed together like normal parents and not broken up so that I wouldn't ever have to think about this stuff. It's not fair. Mum did look a bit sad when she said all that, though (but this was before Dumbledore Chops was around, I have to admit). I didn't want to ask what she meant. I guess I sort of worked it out afterwards anyway – she was saying that Dad loves being drunk more than he loves anything else, I suppose, that he wants to drink more than he wants to be a proper husband or a dad . . . or have a job. That makes me cry. I don't understand how anyone can want to do anything more than love their own kids and do the best for them. I get so angry with Dad when I think about this and all the stuff he's done, or rather not done. He is totally pathetic. I am not going to see him any more. All of this makes me confused. I want them back together but then I don't. If he rings, I'm going to ignore him and then he can just spend all day long drinking if he loves it so much. Loser.

SPRING TERM
WEEK 9

EPIC EVENT ALERT

OMG . . . err . . . oh god . . . it's happened. Well, very nearly happened. I feel so weird. Sort of excited too but majorly weird. My . . . oh my actual god, I can't believe I'm writing this down . . . Aaargh . . . but . . . here goes . . . I think I'm going to start my period.

Yes, I know, can you believe it?! Obviously it is actually believable because I am a girl and I am nearly fourteen years old, and, according to the internet, it's quite old not to have started. So, I'm not saying it's a complete shocker because I had no idea it was going to happen. I am not an idiot. Obvs I knew it was going to happen sometime because that's what happens to girls, derr. I just hadn't thought it would happen now . . . you know . . . before I actually turned fourteen. On the internet it says you can be any age from ten (hello, you'd still be at primary school if that happened – how extra would that be?!) to fourteen, sometimes fifteen. So, I suppose, I'm just about in the middle-middle, which is probably the best time to start, isn't it? Not too young, crazy young like at primary school, and not so old that you're literally the last of your mates to start.

I know Grace has already started hers because she mentioned it at the beginning of term like it was no big deal at all. That is so Grace – we four were sitting around in the playground during break and she pipes up, 'BTW I've started my period, have any of you?' – just like she is saying 'I've finished my sandwich, have you?' Anyway, I haven't actually started, like started-started, but I really think I'm going to any day now. I'm sure of it – my stomach's gone a bit bloaty, which is one definite sign you're going to start your period, according to the internet, and I've had a few weird crampy tummy pains too, and that is number one on the list of 'signs to look out for' and . . . this is a bit embarrassing but . . . this feels well mankenstein to actually write down but here goes: my boobs are a bit tender, something I've deffo never had before. So, you know, if you add all of those 'signs' up then it does sound like I'm going to start, doesn't it?

Aaaargh, I don't really know what I feel – a bit excited, I suppose. It is pretty grown up to actually start your period, plus I defs feel a whole lot nervous. According to the internet, it means I've 'turned into a woman'. Hah! I don't know about that. I mean, for a kick-off, having periods doesn't mean you can suddenly drive a car or go into a pub or leave school, so you're not really a woman, are you? Even so, it is quite exciting. I'm quite pleased if I do start soon that I'm the next in our group at school. That feels pretty good. I definitely wouldn't have wanted to be the last. Oh god, hope I'm not. Fingers crossed it does start soon, although I don't like this bloaty stomach or sore boobs stuff much, I can tell you! I wonder if that happens every single month. What a nightmare if it does. Majorly boring.

I am DEFINITELY NOT going to tell Mum when it does happen. I mean, can you imagine? Knowing her and her determination to 'share' (another one of those words Mum uses to mean something different to what we all think it means — she uses it for spilling her guts in her column, kill me now) every single private thing that ever occurs, and mainly to me, not her. She will probably leap across the room to her computer the moment I tell her and start writing her column, telling everything all about how her 'firstborn' (see what I mean!?) has become a woman or something just as yucky. Bleurgh. So, I am NOT going to tell her when and if it starts. Obvs it's not 'if' . . . I don't think!

With my new pocket money I've bought some just-in-case back-up tampons so that I'm ready. Mum didn't actually say I had to pay for them myself out of my £4 a week, which is just as well because they are SO expensive, but because I don't want to tell her when I start I've got to have these standing by, otherwise I'd have to tell her, wouldn't I? Hmm, thinking about it, I'm obvs going to have to tell Mum at some point soon after I've started otherwise I'll be paying for the tampons myself for ages and then I really won't have a single penny left over.

We've just had supper and get this — I did not bring up the topic of periods. As if. Why would I?! I'm hardly likely to want to chat about the whole thing with my mankenstein little brother, my granny and my mother, am I? I mean, hellooooo, who would? But, out of nowhere, almost as if he knew they'd been on my mind right before supper, Luke says in that super-nerdy I've-got-lots-of-useless-information-stored-up-in-my-brain voice he uses when he's announcing fascinating (not) facts: 'Did you know that scientists have discovered that female rats put in to live together will, within a few months, all share the same menstrual cycles?' Mum and Gran nodded as if to say 'how interesting', but I made a face at him like I thought he was completely mad. He, of course, ignored that and went on: 'And there is some evidence to indicate that human women do the same thing.' Can you believe it? How disgusting and revolting is he?! I was getting all red in the face, I could tell. It just felt like what Luke was really doing was making sure the whole talk at supper was about periods and that somehow they were all going to find out that I am about to start mine. I wanted to scream. Gran laughed and said, 'Well, don't look at me, my periods stopped years ago . . . thank god.' And then Mum said, super caj, as if nothing could be more normal, 'If you're looking to do any trials in this house we'll have to wait for Tabitha's periods to start, then you can see if our cycles fall in together.'

Helloooooo?! My own actual mother actually brought up my periods at the kitchen table, in front of my little brother and while we were eating food as if this was A Completely Normal Thing to do. I could not believe it. I was so embarrassed. I managed to stop myself shouting but I did give Luke a killer look and said, 'If you think I am ever going to tell anyone in this house anything private about myself like that ever you are more of a moron than I already thought you were, so there!' Luke replied, 'Oooh, touchy,' and Mum jumped in, of course, protecting her precious little baby, as per. 'Tabitha, he's just taking an interest in an experiment. You don't need to be so rude.' I completely held myself together, turned to Mum, gave her a really cold stare and said, 'Mum, who I tell what about stuff that only affects me is my business.' Gran said, 'Fair enough,' which obviously really annoyed Mum because she whipped her head round to Gran, who shrugged her shoulders and said, 'Wasn't me. Basil said that,' which did make me laugh. Mum did not laugh. But, seriously, come on. I cannot believe there is one other family on the planet who would ever even contemplate talking about stuff like that all together, never mind while they were eating. It's just my luck to have the craziest, most mankenstein family in the world. Great. I mean, what teenage girl wants to 'share' period time with her own mum?! I literally cannot think of a more embarrassing thing. I don't mean I'm never going to tell Mum anything private but, come on, I cannot believe there is a single normal girl my age who actually wants to diarise her periods with her own mother! I cannot think of a single more mankenstein thing in the world.

BTW I am not saying periods are disgusting or that there is anything wrong with them. Obvs I don't think that. I am a woman. Well, I am a girl who is going to be a woman. One day. Derr. So, I am definitely not saying no one should ever talk about them or pretend they don't happen. I am not an old-fashioned princess. Also, for the record, I don't think there's anything wrong with boys knowing all about them as well. I just don't want my revolting little brother to know all about mine or for my family to be all like, super caj, 'Hey, pass the salt, have you started your period yet?' You know?!

What happens to me and my body is my private

business and I do not want to see it announced in an entry on the family wall-chart calendar, thank you very much!

I reeeeally want to know who else has started their period at school apart from Grace. I don't want to be all like 'Hey, I've started my period' and risk getting a 'So what, everyone else started ages ago' reaction. I know my lot wouldn't say that exactly. They wouldn't be that mean but they might be a bit it's-not-that-big-a deal-ish, mightn't they? Or A'isha might suddenly say something like 'We don't talk about it in my culture', a bit like she was when she thought I was being rude about hijabs. I know she's not like that AT ALL deep down and I know she's one of my absolute bezzies but, you know, you can't always definitely tell when someone, even someone you know really well, is going to suddenly look at you like 'OMG, I can't believe you said that out loud'. And it's not the sort of thing you can bring up just like that, is it? And I definitely do not want to do a Dark Aly.

The whole world knows she's started her period. Last week, and I am not kidding, she put her hand up at the very beginning of class, waited until Miss looked at her and said not quietly at all, in fact, like she was making a big announcement, 'I'm going to medical. I have my period and I don't feel well.' Can you believe it? Of course most of the boys, typically, started sniggering immediately, which, even though I'm not exactly Dark Aly's biggest fan, I did think was totes pathetic. I mean, so what, she has her period? Whoopdeedoo. Okay, she didn't have to say it exactly like that, but if boys had them once a month for their whole lives I'll bet girls wouldn't snigger. Also, everyone knows boys would talk about them all the time. Oh, but get this, Miss, who was obviously a bit surprised that Dark Aly had been so out there said, 'Yes, all right, off you go. I don't think we all need to know the details.' Dark Aly scraped her chair back really, really slowly to get up. (I'll bet she got that off me; that's exactly what I do when I get up in class because it always drives the teachers crazy!) Then she stared straight at Miss and said, 'I disagree. I think this is a subject that everyone should discuss, male or female – without periods there is no human race.' Can you actually believe it?! That is exactly what she said! How extra is that?! The whole class was, like, OMG, totes shocked. That certainly shut the boys' sniggering up too.

Grace whispered to me, 'She's got a point.' Of course it would be Grace that agreed with her. I don't not agree with her but I would never ever do what she did. She might have wanted to Make A Point but that was totes random.

I do not like admitting this but it was sort of brave of Dark Aly, wasn't it? Random, extra and way bonkers, for def, but a bit brave too, don't you think?

SPRING TERM
WEEK 9

PUPPY LUUURVE

So, in the end, basics, we called Basil's baby – erm, hold on, wait a minute, you don't say baby for a dog, do you? Obvs I know you say 'puppy' but then that doesn't sound like it's actually Basil's own 'child', does it? Anyway, whatevs, I'm talking about the puppy we got off Sam's mum (eventually, after she realised how horrible she'd been to Gran when Gran said she wanted them, way back). You know, the puppies Basil had . . . erm . . . 'fathered' (what a mankenstein word!) with Bonnie, Sam's dog. Well, the puppy who is here, living with us, is called Scramble. Isn't that the bestest name ever? He is NOT called Scrabble as, guess who (of course, Luke) wanted to call him. I mean, purleeze, Scrabble? We might as well have called him Swotty or Homework or just gone straight for it and called him Nerd. Hah, hah, that's actually quite funny – can you imagine calling out for your dog if it was called Nerd?! That would be hilar but, thinking about it, although it would be a really funny name, you could only call it that if there was no chance ever, like in a kertrillion years, that anyone would hear the dog's name and then look at you and think, *Well*, you *are the nerd*. Anyway, seeing as it's mainly me who walks the dogs, well, Basil and his . . . son . . . can you say that? . . . I got the final say over name. Huh, for a change. It's usually always Crybaby Luke who gets the final say on practically everything because 'He's the youngest, so it's only fair', according to Mum. Anyway, because this puppy is always scampering about all over the shop I've called him Scramble. I didn't want to call him Scamper, which was Mum's lame and oh-so-obvious suggestion. It sounds like the name a dog would be called in a silly old-fashioned pigtails-and-jolly-hockey-sticks type of book! I reckon Scramble is much more original and hip. Like Scrambled Eggs, although he doesn't look like them!

Anyway, when you say Scramble it makes me think of things being scrumptious, which is good because I've got to admit he is the sweetest little thing you have ever seen in your whole life. He's as white as fresh snow and sooooo fluffy and tiny. He's not so much a puppy as a warm hand towel! You could deffo dry your face with him. And when he trots about on his little legs he picks his paws up really, really quickly in between steps — it looks like he's doing a dance on a hot plate — it is THE cutest thing and absolutely killingly funny. Luke and I cannot stop laughing every time he does it. And Scramble doesn't mind at all. I think he actually does it more when we're laughing. And, get this, he even manages to look adorable in all the stuff Gran's been knitting for him.

Yes, correct, Gran is, of course, knitting mini things for him to wear too, and, wait for it, they're identical to all Basil's stuff so I have to take them out for their walks in matching outfits! But I don't really mind any more. And Scramble is so dinky he'd look good in anything you put him in, even a dirty old plastic bag! And I'm so used to Basil's bonkers outfits I've stopped worrying about them too. I think I used to care as much as I did mainly because I was worried about what Sam would think of me when he saw me with a dog wearing a knitted beret or a tank top or a coatigan (that was defs the worst!). Obvs Sam did mention the outfits when we first met but he doesn't so much any more and he's never been mean about them. I mean, come on, you'd have to be crazy *not* to think it was a teensy bit odd for a dog to be wearing a knitted beret.

Now, Sam . . . yeah, hmm, interesting one this. So, remember he got my number or re-got my number because he'd lost his phone, after he'd brought round the puppies, Scramble and the other one Gran so nicely gave to Dad's mum GB to stop her trying to make me live with her? Well, he did text quite soon after that and we met at the cinema a couple of times. But NOTHING HAPPENED. I'm not saying I really wanted something to happen. Well, not something specific, you know. It's not as if I had something in my head that defs had to happen. I wasn't actually hoping and planning for something boyfriend-girlfriend-y to happen. I'm not like madly in love with him or anything extra like that. I don't know, I just sort of thought once we'd actually done a few things alone, just us, it might feel different, more . . . I don't know, just more . . . more, like, different! So, we are most defs not dating. We are NOT boyfriend and girlfriend, no matter what Luke says, thinking he's being so hilarious. My gang, Emz, A'isha and Grace – well, not Grace, because she doesn't 'speculate' as she loves to say. I know, random or what. But anyway the other two reckon Sam is 'taking his time' and is probably a bit shy about doing anything that might make me go 'Eeurgh, yuck,' but I don't know.

I'm not saying having a boyfriend is mankenstein BTW. I'm just saying I don't know if it would be for me right now. I don't even know for defs that I actually want Sam as my boyfriend. I'm not saying I want someone else as a boyfriend. There is no one else. I mean, maybe Sam is going to be my actual boyfriend one day. I don't know. Like on Facebook I guess I don't, right now, put 'in a relationship' under relationship status, do I? Can't do that anyway because everyone would see it and make a massive big deal about it . . . Oh man, I hate all this having to think about it and plan it and then say what it is and then tell everyone that this person, whoever, Is My Boyfriend. It's all so extra and announce-y.

Obvs Emz, A'isha, Grace and me talk about boys we like from school. It's not like we're all wannabe nuns, but, you know, we're not obsessed with them, I don't think. We're not all in a mad, crazy rush to Have A Boyfriend like some girls at school. Oh man, some of them are so extra, so obvious, just like totes obsessed with boys and they go all stupid and giggly and wriggly (random or what?!) when the fittest ones are nearby. Losers. I am never going to do that. It's so pathetic and makes them look like they think Boys Are The Best. Well, I've got one at home, and I can tell you Boys Are SO Not The Best! I am going to have a boyfriend one day, of course, but he will not be like Luke in any single way, even if it is Sam. And I am never going to giggle and wriggle and go all gooey and swoony when he's around. That is just pathetic.

I see Sam most days when I walk Basil and Scramble and we usually end up walking our dogs together, which is nice and easy and pretty much what, I think, we both sort of expect to do now. See? Does that mean we're a couple? I don't think so, not really. Emz and A'isha do but how can you tell? It's not like anyone comes up to you and says, 'Oh, BTW, FYI, we are now A Couple, just so you know,' do they? And if they did that would be so lame and embarrassing.

Anyway, it is so boring walking the dogs alone, so even though I don't know what it means (assuming it means anything!) I prefer walking with Sam. I never know what to think about when I'm on my own! So, that's four dogs we're walking when we walk together.

It's practically impossible to fit on the pavement! The good thing is you can't take little puppies like Scramble and Kiki (that is what Sam's mum has called their puppy; she's a girl – not at all sure about that name!) for as long walks as older dogs like Basil and Bonnie; their tiny little legs can't take it! Even Sam's noticed Scramble's funny little dancey walk. He said, 'That's not walking, it's trotting, have you been teaching him dressage?' I laughed because he was obviously trying to be funny, even though I had no idea what dressage was.

Looked up dressage when I got home. The idea of tiny little Scramble being taught to do horsey prancing about made me laugh out loud. Sam is funny.

Oh god, I can't believe it, what a stupid cretin I am! I showed Gran the pic on my phone I'd taken of Kiki because she is super cute and looks exactly like Scramble, her brother after all (can you say brother and sister for sibling dogs?!) and I knew Gran would love to see her. But I didn't think! I should have guessed!

Gran, of course, derr, took one look and said, 'Ooh, she's very sweet but she'll be even sweeter in a sweater,' and then laughed, obvs because she thought 'sweeter in a sweater' sounded funny. I suppose it does, a bit, but all I could think was 'aaaaargh'. That means Gran is going to knit things for Kiki and I am going to have to take them to Sam and he will have to make her wear them because Gran will want a photo!!!!!!!!!!

I absolutely totes adore Gran, of course I do, but, come on, it's one thing deciding to dress your own dog and puppy up in bonkers knitted things, because, you know, they're your dogs and you can pretty much do what you like (apart from be cruel to them, obvs) but it's a bit random – no, it's way random – to expect other people to dress their dogs up in that stuff too! But I can't tell Gran I don't want to do it or that Sam's not going to want to either. I just can't. That's partly because the thing is, and this sort of makes me want to cry a bit, I don't think it's ever once even occurred to Gran that the outfits aren't just totes amazeballs and gorgeous and that everyone in the world who loves dogs wouldn't want to dress them like that too.

Just about to go to sleep. At supper Gran was going on about how adorable Kiki was and how she can't wait to knit girly things for her. Kill me now. Even Luke made an 'oh no' face at me.

I've been thinking about what Gran thinks about the outfits sort of nearly making me cry. That feels a bit weird. But it's a bit like when Dad says he misses us and wishes things were different – that makes me want to cry too sometimes, but mainly it makes me angry because with Dad of course things *could* be different – if he wasn't an alky! Dad should not say to me, his daughter, 'I wish things were different' because he *did* have something to do with how things are now. Grr. Next time he says that I'm deffo going to say to him something like, 'Well, if you *wish* things were different then why don't you actually DO something instead of wishing?' It's time someone said something to him. I don't want to hear him moaning any more. God, if I was like that at school I'd get such a row. 'Miss, I wish I could do my homework better . . .' That is quite funny. Maybe I'll try it out soon. The teacher would so not know what to say. Hilar.

About Gran, though, I don't know, it's like I can't bear to think of Gran thinking something that no one else thinks. I know this sounds a bit out there but it sort of feels like other people might be laughing at Gran and she doesn't know it. Well, I can't have that. I'm going to take whatever Gran knits for Kiki and not let a single muscle in my face move if Sam or his mum say anything. I'm going to pretend I think whatever outfit she knits, no matter how bonkers, is absolutely fantastic and not at all weird for a puppy to wear. Inside I can think whatever I like but on the outside I am going to be like 'this is THE best thing ever'. No one is going to laugh at my gran.

Still can't decide whether to have a party or not. I mainly want to. It's just the whole eggy look-at-me factor that's making me not sure . . . Could be a real laugh, though.

SPRING TERM WEEK 10

A MAJORLY BAD THING

So, we're in science with Mr Proctor, this morning, aka Mr Proper, you know, because he's so ridic over-the-top strict, when he announces he's giving us some major project to complete by the end of this term. Blah, blah, blah, so what, who cares? BUT then he says the project has got to be done in pairs, but I'm like not thinking and not bothered about it and TBH not really listening when I suddenly realise Grace isn't in our set for this subject and that you can't get a pair out of Emz, A'isha and me, because we are three! A pair is most defs two people. I don't panic at first but then I notice that Mr Proper has already started writing up pairs of names on the whiteboard and he's put Emz and A'isha in a pair and then me – and you will NOT believe this! – in a pair with Dark Aly!!!! I am not joking. And the thing is everyone knows Mr Proper is SO not one of the kind of teachers you can reason with or even ask if you can do anything at all differently to how he's decided it has to be. He's like it is my way or no way. So extra and totes ridic.

I nearly burst into tears I was so upset. Obvs I couldn't actually do that, though. My mind was whizzing, thinking of how I could get out of this. I mean, come on, doing a project, which means spending loads of time on it outside of class etc. etc. is bad enough, but doing it with Dark Aly?! Emz and A'isha both made 'aaaargh' faces at me but they weren't taking it that seriously at all and, I could see, thought it was a bit funny that I was paired up with her. I suppose I might have thought it was funny too if it hadn't been happening to me. But this situ was so bad I wasn't all 'aaaargh' back at them, like we usually all are when something bad happens. This was way too serious for a group 'aaaargh', which, I admit, does usually crack us up and make the thing that made us go 'aaaargh' in the first place seem not that bad at all. But I was all, like, there is NO WAY this is going to happen. Over my dead body do I team up with that grumpy goth. As if.

But then, and this is so random, I looked over at Dark Aly, who I thought would be as annoyed as I was about the idea of us being forced to pair up, especially as we're not even mates at all, but she smiled at me — well, smiled as much as any goth ever smiles, so, you know, a sort of snarl-slash-smile-slash-lipcurl, your basic Goth Smile. It was almost like she was actually pleased this had happened! I was really surprised and a bit freaked out TBH. It never occurred to me she might be okay about working with me, or anyone. I was sure she'd have a major strop, the kind she is always having when teachers tell her to do practically anything, even the tiniest thing. Dark Aly always goes out of her way to work on her own. She makes a big, usually scarily, big deal of telling teachers she will never, her word, 'collaborate'. I am not joking, that is seriously what she says. But here she was looking like she didn't mind 'collaborating' with me one bit, apparently. How extra is that?

At first I was worried that it might be a trick, like she was pretending to be all 'yeah, fine, super, what fun, Tab and me can team up' and then as soon as I walked over she was going to have some huge meltdown, screaming and yelling at Mr Proper about him 'not respecting her need for solitude' or 'attempting to force his drone-like working practices on her'. (For real, she really does say things like this!) So, in case she was planning on doing something out there like that, I stayed where I was, at our table, and just nodded at her, sort of to say 'Yeah, all right, I get it. We're working together on this project, big deal'. But I made absolutely sure it was a really quick nod so that she deffo couldn't suddenly decide it meant I was all golly-gosh-super-keen-can't-wait-to-work-with-you or anything extra like that.

Once Mr Proper had finished writing up all the pairs he handed out sheets with the project's title on them:

'An Example of Science at Work in Society' (erm, hellooo, what?!). And then he said he expected us to 'organise yourselves in your own time in order to complete the project satisfactorily'. Great, so not only do I have to work with Dark Aly but he is obviously expecting us to work on it in our own time. Extra or what? And, on top of all that, I have absolutely no idea what that means and there is no way I'm letting Dark Aly know that.

I was with Emz and A'isha, who were really annoyingly teasing me about having to work with Dark Aly, which they obviously still found hilarious (nice), and just as we walked through the door, out of class, I heard Aly say my name, well, grunt it, which is how she speaks. Emz and A'isha looked at me and said, 'See you in the canteen,' and went off. I was a bit cross that they didn't wait, but I don't suppose they really could have hung around because then it would have looked like I was frightened to be alone with the goth.

'So, could be quite interesting this project, don't you think?' she said, quite friendly-ly for her. 'Yeah, I suppose so,' I replied. I wasn't trying to be deliberately horrible or anything. I was just a bit worried that she might have some random reaction up her sleeve. Plus I was nervous of her thinking I was way keen and giving her the chance to suddenly take the mick. Anyway, when am I ever keen on schoolwork, hello?!

'You know what the project is, don't you?' Dark Aly then asked. Obvs there was no way I was going to admit I didn't, so I shrugged my shoulders, sort of making out I did. 'If we have to do a science project this is a good one because really it just means find anything that happens in life that you can prove through science, like . . . I dunno . . . the majority of football hooligans are male or only females can have children. We just need to pick a fact we'd be interested in writing about.'

I was so relieved she'd explained it, but couldn't say that so I nodded again and said, 'Right.' And then she didn't say anything else so I said, 'All right, well, I'll see you later.' I didn't want to say I was going to the canteen to meet my lot in case she tried to come with. She probably wouldn't ever do that but, you know . . . and anyway it's a bit mean to say you're going off to meet other people from the same class and not ask them to come along, isn't it? And I don't want to be actually horrible to Dark Aly. It's not like I want to be bezzies with her either, but, if we've got to do this project together (and because it's for Mr Proper we have GOT to), then it's probably best if we can get on all right. As I walked off she called after me: 'You know what, because it's us two, we should do this really well, that'd show Sir, wouldn't it?! And then she laughed and walked off in the opposite direction. Random or what?

This is weird, but I think she actually wants to be friends. I'm not being big-headed or saying I'm so great or anything, even though I am still the coolest girl in Year 9 (I must be, two Year 10 boys nodded at me in the hall the other day and I have never even spoken to them!), but I just got this feeling that she's sort of secretly pleased that she's been forced to pair up with me. I know she'd never in a gerzillion years be caught actually trying to make an effort to be friends or work with anyone else. As if. Oh man, she wouldn't be caught dead doing that. But this way she was put with me without having to say that that was what she actually wanted. Does that make sense? TBH, I can really understand that, especially after she'd set herself up as this scary don't-talk-to-me sulky goth right from day one. I mean, you can't exactly be like that and then suddenly be all 'Hey, can we be mates?', can you? Because now that she's been here for nearly two terms and she really doesn't have any mates, just like she apparently wanted, it's sort of a bit late for her to start trying to make them, isn't it?

So, you know, I'm not like going to get her to join our gang or anything extra like that but I am going to just see how it goes when we do the project. I am going to have what Gran calls 'an open mind'. Hah, soooo me, eh?!

Just about to go to sleep but wanted to say this project does sound like you can choose anything you want as long as it's science-y, so we could do something really interesting — hey, maybe even funny. I mean, because it's us two doing it we'll choose something really random that defs no one else would choose. Can't believe I'm saying this but I'm actually sort of looking forward to it. Extra or what?!

Might not tell my gang that. Well, not yet. Don't want them thinking I've suddenly turned into a Super Nerd. I've got a rep to keep up after all!

So, asked my lot and everyone thinks I should have a party — of course! Hmm, mainly thinking I will but still not totes sure . . . aaargh.

SPRING TERM
WEEK 10

GCSES!!!

OH, MY ACTUAL GOD! Aaaargh! What am I going to do?! Raaaats, poo, boo, poo and, just, in fact, double aaaaaaargh! You are not going to believe this. Literally, it is so totes ridic it is impossible to believe. Right, so, it's the GCSE options evening next week and, wait for it, Dad has said he's going to come along. He hasn't actually told me, because I'm not speaking to him, although he doesn't seem to have realised that yet. Derr. He keeps leaving me voice-mails saying things like 'Oh, we keep missing each other, darling, ring me when you can'. And then when I don't he leaves another message like that.

Doesn't he get it?! I am not talking to him. Well, for now.

Anyway, so he sent me a text saying he'd got a letter from school about the GCSE options and he was going to make a 'special trip up' so he could be there. Kill me now. Just literally, actually, kill me now. I cannot do this. I cannot have my dad AND my mum meeting my teachers TOGETHER. Or, in fact, my dad meeting my teachers EVER with or without Mum there. They have split up. That is that. I cannot have any of my friends or teachers even catching sight of my dad. Ever. Dad lives with his mum, GB, in the country. You know, like a Loser. At his mum's house he drinks all day long because, apparently, 'he can't cope'. Extra Loser. Mum, who is super annoying but at least manages not to drink all day long, and my brother and me now live in London with Gran. And that is that too. And it's been like this for ages. So, where does Dad get off suddenly thinking it's okay for him to have a go at being A Proper Dad and come to my school to, his words, 'help me choose my GCSEs'? And with Mum?! It is literally the worst idea in the world. And, get this, Mum doesn't even seem to mind. She actually said to me, 'It's up to Dad, I guess.' I can't believe she doesn't mind him being there. It is NOT up to him; it's up to me. It's my life, my GCSEs, my school, my friends, my teachers. And what if Dad's been drinking that day?! It is going to be the most embarrassing, awful, cringe-worthy night of my entire life. Even if he has managed to not have a drink it's still going to be HORRIBLE.

I'd forgotten the school sends out all letters to both parents when they're split up. But it's SO not like him. He never did things like that even when he and Mum were together. Why's he trying it out now? It's a bit late for all this 'look at me, I am being A Good Dad' act. Dad hasn't got the first clue about what I like and want to do; he's going to be useless as well as embarrassing!

I've worked it out. It won't have been Dad's idea. As If. Dad's mum, GB, will have read the letter and come up with this brilliant, not, plan to prove that her precious boy is A Good Dad. Even if I wanted him there I think it probably takes a bit more than one trip to prove you're A Good Parent. Ridic.

I know, I won't go! I'll just refuse to go to my GCSE options eve. Hah. Dad can go with Mum. See how he likes that! Oh god, I can't do that because then how will I choose my options? There's no way I can say to the school: 'Can I choose them on my own in case my dad embarrasses me?' They'd make me explain why and what the matter was and then I'd have to say what was wrong with Dad and that would be excruciating, or worse they might not actually believe me and, oh man, then say something to him! No, I can't not go or speak to school. It's way too risky.

I'm going to have to talk to Grace about this. She'll know what to do. Sometimes it's so useful having a swotty, nerdy pal. I'm not being mean, that's what she calls herself. Anyway, she's not a nerd-nerd. She's just more of a think-y type than I am.

DUMBLEDORE
CHOPS

← NOT A COOL
BEARD

As if things aren't bad enough right now with this whole nightmare, to make sure my life is completely ruined Dumbledore Chops was here at supper AGAIN. (Why doesn't he just move in if he loves it so much?! Oh god, no, please don't let that happen. It would be THE WORST.)

After he'd left — he never stays over, which is the best thing about him. Can you imagine how totes mankenstein it would be if he stayed here, with Mum, in Mum's room? Pass the sick bucket. I'd run away (again but for real this time) if he did. Actually, thinking about it, Mum's never stays out, you know, at his for the night either . . . maybe they don't . . . Aargh, not going to think about THAT. Bleurgh. Anyway, after he'd gone I heard Mum on the phone talking to one of her boring mates. And she went on for ages. Whoever was on the other end of the phone seemed, unbelievably, to be interested because Mum kept going on about the price of a tin of tomatoes. They were obviously having an actual conversation about it. How extra is that? That has to be the BORINGEST conversation anyone in the world has ever had IN THE HISTORY OF TIME.

If I ever had a conversation like that I know I'd just die. Literally die. Like literally kill me now die. The stuff my mates and me talk about is always interesting. We've always got masses to talk about, masses.

I hope, for her sake (and mine, though, mainly obvs), Mum does not write about stuff like that in her column. If she does, no one is ever going to read it again. Actually, do you know what, I'm going to tell her, just in case she does think about going on about that stuff when she writes. It's one thing if it's between her and her mates. At least they know her and, sounds like, agree with her that stuff as incredibly uninteresting as that is worth talking about, but she mustn't inflict it on strangers.

Okay, so I've just been downstairs to tell Mum not to write about that sort of who-cares-stuff in her column. I was trying to be nice, help her out, so, you know, she wouldn't look like a complete idiot. I was really nice and said I wasn't trying to be horrible, just trying to give her some advice and do you know what she did? She literally laughed out loud and for ages too. I was like 'have you gone off your head?' and then eventually she said, 'Darling, I'm sure the stuff you and your pals talk about is fascinating to you now but when you're my age you'll find different things interesting.' And then didn't promise NOT to write about it.

She'd better not write about that stuff in her column or it'll all be over and she will not like that. Hmm, actually I won't like it either because it's deffo true that Mum's been much happier since she got the column and since it's doing well and everything. NOT that she seems to have got any more money because of it, or so she says.

SPRING TERM WEEK 10

THE POO THAT WOULDN'T DIE!

Ooh, you'll never guess what! This is so exciting. So I was walking to school doing the whole 'if three buses pass before I get to the corner then I will have my party but if it's less then I won't' thing and then I noticed that the tatty old place that used to be a dry cleaner's or something like that, which has been shut for literally ages, like even before we moved here, had builders in it and a sign up in the window that said 'real coffee made by real people with real love – coming soon'. Okay, that's all a bit hippy-dippy as far as I'm concerned because what does 'real people' mean? They couldn't exactly open a coffee shop with fake people, could they? Then it would be a vending machine! But anyway the main thing is that it means there's going to be a trendy coffee shop really near my house. Yay! I know I don't drink coffee yet but I am so going to hang out there. And I'll meet Emz and A'isha and Grace there too. Oh man, it's going to be so great. And my house is the nearest to it out of everyone's so it'll be like 'my place'. Kind of. I LOVE that. It's so kind of New York-y, isn't it?

The place was being all kitted out with really cool tables made of floorboards, and random chairs, like not all matching, and loads of light bulbs all hanging down from the ceiling at different heights but with no shades. It looks so incredibly cool. And with the builders was a woman, a really young one, who was doing stuff too – wouldn't it be great if she turns out to be the owner? When I stopped to read the sign she gave me a really big smile and waved at me, which I think is a bit weird as I've never seen her before in my life, but I guess it was nice too. I hope they do other stuff too, not just coffee, I've tasted it a couple of times and I don't like it at all, but I so want to hang out in there.

During break we all talked about my party again and if I should have one and who should be invited etc. etc. and everyone decided I defs should. At first I was thinking, *Oh great, yeah, of course you all think I should do it but it's not going to be at yours, is it?* But then I realised I was probably being a bit silly. They were all just like 'Yay, a party, that's going to be so fab'. None of us have had a party since I came to HAC, I realised, so it is kind of cool to be the first (not like with periods, though!). And then everyone started talking about what sort of party it should be. All the ideas were a bit samey, so I, super super caj so that I wouldn't look all like it was something I'd been planning my whole entire life, told them about Mum's 'mocktail' suggestion and, amazeballs, everyone thought it was a fantastic idea! 'Oh my god, then that means we can all wear cocktail dresses!' Emz said, all excited. 'Oh yeah, how cool would that be?' A'isha squealed, jumping up. I was about to ask if she'd still wear her hijab with that sort of dress but then quickly decided I'd better not in case it was a really stupid question or I offended her. But then A'isha said, 'But I'm going to have to change at one of yours – can you imagine Dad catching me in a cocktail dress with my hijab?! Ridic. Oh man, his Messed-up-Muslim radar would literally explode!' We all laughed out loud. She can be so funny, especially when she's imitating her dad. We're never laughing at A'isha's dad, though. Well, I'm not and I don't think anyone else is. He's really nice. We're laughing at how random his decisions are about what makes A'isha 'a good Muslim girl'. Like one day he told her she couldn't do PE and then suddenly he's all: 'Why aren't you in the girls' football club?' Crazy. And double crazy because none of us would ever join that club, anyway, even if we totes loved PE. As if. You have to stay after school twice a week to do training even when there are no matches. I mean, hellooooo, extra or what?

So, I'm quite excited about the party now, especially because my bezzies are too. That way it doesn't feel like it's only me looking forward to it and worrying about how it will be. Does that make sense? We all decided it should be just us four, obvs, and a few others from our class because otherwise it's not really like a party, is it? But I don't know who else to invite. I'm only inviting girls. I don't want boys there. If I invite boys then it gets too stressy and not as much fun because you have to worry about how the boys are going to be. Not Dark Aly, I don't think. I mean, I know I'm going to do that project with her now, thanks to Mr Proper, but for a kick-off can you imagine her, major goth, wearing a cocktail dress?! And we're not mates so it'd be a bit weird to invite her. I know Gran, and, actually Grace, probably, would say I ought to but it's my party and I think it would be all eggy if I did. I'll bet she'd give me a really long stare-y look, like she thought I was totes pathetic, and then after ages of looking at me like that she'd say something like 'What makes you think I would want to celebrate your birthday with you?' or else deffo something that would just make me want to die on the spot and get really angry and super regret asking her. Anyhoo, don't know why I'm worrying about how Dark Aly's going to be if I invite her to my party because I am not going to do that!

I wonder if Mum will buy me a new dress for the party. Hmm, she'd better not try to say 'Yes, but it's your present'! I hate it when parents and other grown-ups try to turn things you actually *need* into presents. Like last Christmas Mum gave me a rucksack, which I did really want, but it was for school too, and she insisted it was my main present and, get this, said, 'It's your choice if you take it to school. It is not a school bag per-say (what?!), therefore it is a present.' Luke was loving it because, of course, he, being a super nerd, had carefully listed every single thing he wanted and because he is so completely uncool then there was no fear for him of any of his presents being 'for school' because everything he wants was to do with learning, reading and generally being a major swot. Lucky him.

I must make sure Luke is NOT in for my party. Or Mum. Or Gran. Or Basil and Scramble. Actually those two can be there because Scramble is so adorable and he'll love it and will probably dance about and make everyone laugh but everyone else in my family has to be out. That's fair enough, isn't it? I don't think I'm being, as Mum keeps saying, 'unreasonable', am I? But, whatever happens, Luke defs cannot be there. He is eleven now and just gets more and more mankenstein every single minute that he's alive.

LUKE

You are not going to believe this. I actually, actually could not believe it when it happened. It is literally the most disgusting, most mankenstein thing that has ever happened in the history of mankosity, like, legit. So, do you know what he did? I can't believe I'm writing this down but I'm going to prove how totes revolting he is. A few days ago we were all in, just sort of hanging around. I was in my room, so obvs I didn't know (or care!) exactly where everyone else was, when I heard Luke shouting really loudly, 'Mum, come and look at this! It's enormous. It won't go down! I need help! Help me!' She didn't come up immediately, because you could tell from his voice, even though he was shouting, it wasn't like the house was on fire or anything. Eventually I went out to have a look because he kept on and on shouting 'help!' like a loon and found him in the bathroom, yes, my bathroom, or the one I wish was my bathroom. He was standing right next to the loo looking down into it (the same loo I have told him one million times he can't use because of his total inability to aim his pee actually into it rather than all over the seat, which is what he always does!!). Before I had a chance to ask him what he was on about, Mum came rushing in. 'What on earth's the matter?' she said, but, of course, because it was Luke she wasn't all irritated like she'd have been if I'd shouted like that for that long. 'Look,' Luke said, pointing right into the loo, 'this poo won't flush. It's so big it won't go down!

I've flushed loads!' I am not joking, *that* is what he was shouting about. And do you know what? Mum burst out laughing and then walked off still laughing and called over her shoulder, 'Leave it for a bit. It'll soften and then go down.'

I was speechless. I could not believe she'd laughed. Luke had screamed for her to come up and help like he was in proper, actual trouble! And she thought it was funny! We all know what would have happened if I'd done that! She would literally never ever have stopped going on about it. It is so incredibly unfair and so completely obvious that he is defs her favourite and that was rock-solid proof — she even thinks what comes out of his bum is special and interesting!

I wonder if all boys do things like that? Or maybe it's just my annoying little brother? Did Dad do things like that when he was young? YUCK. Does Sam do things like that? I can't believe he would. I read once about a bunch of boys all lighting each other's farts because, apparently, if you do that the air from the fart makes a huge blue flame. Big deal. Whoopdeedoo. I mean, I admit seeing a flame come out of someone's bottom would be quite cool, but you'd probably have to hang around near their bum hole waiting for it and who the hell wants to do that?! I suppose boys, that's who. I'll bet no girl anywhere in the world has ever done that or shown anyone, ever, their big poo in the loo. No matter how gigantic and unflushable it was. Oh, that's quite funny, actually: big poo in the loo. I am going to call Luke Big Poo In The Loo from now on. Hah, hah, that'll make him sorry he did it. That is so brilliant – Big Poo In The Loo. I'm going to start at supper tonight. 'Hey, Big Poo In The Loo, can you pass the bread, please?' 'When are you getting the uniform for your new swots-only school, Big Poo In The Loo?' I am never going to let him forget this. He's going to regret inviting everyone to look at his too-big-to-flush turd for the rest of his life. At his wedding I'll make a speech about it! Not that anyone is ever going to want to marry him. As if.

SPRING TERM WEEK 10

WEDNESDAY

PARTAAY ON DOWN

So, Mum says I can have ten people for my party including me, so that's nine not-mes. I was a bit surprised, actually, because I was sure Mum was going to say something like 'Five is fine' or something totes lame and ridic like that. But I think ten is okay, isn't it? It's actually quite a good number. It won't look totes empty and like I've got no mates. It should look like I'm quite popular, especially because our living room, if you include the kitchen that is sort of part of it, is so small ten of us in there is going to be jam-packed. I'm not absolutely sure who I'm going to invite. I'll have to ask the others what they think but this is my list, so far.

List of people to invite for my party
Me — defs, obvs!
Emz — defs, obvs!
A'isha — defs, obvs!
Grace — defs, obvs!
Lily B — semi-defs
Lily O — hmm, semi-defs
Maya — I'll defs invite her. She's really nice, even though we don't hang around with her much.
Nell — she's Maya's bezzie so I guess she has to be a defs.
Ella — hmm, not sure about her, she's quite snobby, I think. I don't know her that well but I don't want to risk her being snooty about Gran's house or anything.
Molly — she's a laugh, so defs.

Back-ups — just in case any of that other lot can't come
Emma — she's a bit quiet, so I'll only invite her if someone else can't make it.

Anoushka — I don't really like her much but Grace does, so she's a maybe but deffo not a defs-defs.

I've been looking at cocktail dresses on the internet. You can get some really fab ones. I don't want one that's got a sticky-out skirt, though, like a tutu, and is all super girly, but it'd be nice to have something that looked like the real thing. Assuming Mum agrees to buy me one at all, and not as my birthday present. I just know she's going to say it has to be wearable after my party, i.e. not for that one time so that I can, wait for it, 'justify the expense'. How completely typical of a grown-up to say something as ridic as that. I mean, if the cost of every single thing you wear has to be divided by how many times you wear it so that you can work out how many pounds each 'wear' costs then you might as well go around in your dressing gown all day or a horrible pair of second-hand trousers because that would be the only real way of 'justifying the expense', wouldn't it? Mum is always going on about 'getting value for money' but you can't talk about value for money when you're talking about clothes, can you? Honestly, sometimes I think Mum knows absolutely nothing about the real world, and most defs not the actual world I live in!

BTW I'm not doing invitations, you know card ones, for my party. I'm not six! Actual invitations are a bit babyish, I think, you know, and a bit extra as in look-at-me-I'm-making-a-huge-big-deal-about-this. I'll just invite the people on my deffo list and then send them a text afterwards with the address and time and all that when (if!) they say yes. That's way cooler, isn't it? And also it won't look like I've made the most mammoth effort of all time for the party, which I so don't want.

So, at school, in Mr Proper's class he made us get into the pairs to start talking about the project. Of course I realised immediately that this meant going to sit with Dark Aly but as if that weren't bad enough as soon he announced this Emz and A'isha starting making stupid faces at me like they were saying 'OMG, you've got to go and sit with Dark Aly now!' It's not like I didn't know that was going to happen anyway so it wasn't exactly super helpful them making faces about it seconds before I had to actually do it. Thanks a lot.

Dark Aly had obviously been thinking about it loads, which is just as well because I hadn't at all TBH. As if. I know I'd said I'd been looking forward to it but, you know, I haven't had time to think about it since. Now I can only say this here – well, so far. I could tell Grace because she won't go all sarky and 'Ooh, is she your new bezzie then?' like I just know Emz and A'isha will if I tell them this – but Dark Aly's idea for the project is actually really good. What she suggested is that we make a list of all the things that happen at school outside of lessons and then 'observe' (her word obvs!) which ones girls and boys mainly do – not like football but more like things anyone could do (I know girls can do football but none of them actually do, probably because the boys hog the balls and the pitch so we never get a chance).

I must admit I didn't really get what she was talking about at first, but after a bit I did. Basics we're going to make a chart of about eight things — like who sits where in the canteen at lunchtime, who goes outside, who uses the library etc. etc. You know all the things at school you can actually choose whether you do them or not, and then we'll see if you can tell if more boys do some things than girls and vice versa. Cool, huh? I'm not sure exactly what that's going to all mean but we can decide that after we've worked it all out. I'm so glad Dark Aly came up with something like that because it's quite random and pretty cool and I'll bet nothing like what anyone else chooses.

Oh yeah, I'm going to stop calling her Dark Aly. I obvs can't call her that to her face and if I keep saying it to my gang then I might accidentally say it to her when we're doing the project together. So, I'll just call her Aly from now. I'm not being mean but I'm secretly quite pleased we're supposed to do this project in our own time, mainly because I don't really want to start sitting with her in all Mr Proper's classes. I want to stay with my bezzies and that's okay, isn't it?

I was really nervous about asking people to my party and nearly didn't, but then I thought, *If I don't there's no party, derr.* So I just sort of went for it. So, as school was finishing and we were all hanging about in the playground before we left I asked, well, more like caj mentioned, my party to the girls on the defs list and amazeballs, massive phew, everyone said yes straight away without one second of looking like they were thinking, *Oh god, what am I going to say? How embarrassing, I so don't want to go to her lame party,* which TBH I was sort of dreading. I don't think any one of them would really think that but you never really know and of all the things in the world having a party deffo makes you suddenly feel like that's what people are maybe going to think. Only Ella said she'd have to check with her mum, which I don't think was an excuse . . . because, if you think about it, if you were trying to get out of something the first thing you'd say wouldn't be that you had to check with your mum. That makes you look pathetic. So I reckon it must have been true.

Oh yeah and everyone really loved the idea of it being a 'mocktail party' too, so that made me feel really pleased . . . and relieved! I'm obvs not going to tell Mum, though. She'll probably only start going on about how brilliant she was for having such a fantastic idea, blah, blah, blah. I mean, I know it was actually her idea but it's not like she invented it or anything major like that!

SPRING TERM
WEEK 10 (THURSDAY)

ANNOYING SECRET MESSAGES

When I got back from school you will never believe what was on my bed, just lying there, no note, nothing, just sitting there like a huge embarrassing, stupid thing that had landed from another planet — a packet of . . . Oh man, I don't want to say it . . . sanitary towels! Oh, my actual god, I wanted to die on the spot. I knew Mum had put them there. That is exactly the sort of thing she does without knowing anything about what's going on with me. Not that long ago she left a pamphlet in exactly the same place, supposedly written for teenagers, called WHEN PARENTS SPLIT

UP. She didn't say anything or even talk about it later – she just left it there. I didn't read it. I flicked through it and it was so moronic and so obviously written by a grown-up who knew nothing, so I chucked it away but see what I mean? That sort of supposedly secret message is so typical of Mum and super annoying.

Anyway, so here was her latest so-called 'helpful hint' lying on my bed. It felt like they were screaming out 'Look at me, your mum thinks you've started your period so we're here to help!!!' I picked them up and stormed downstairs. 'What the hell are these doing on my bed?' I shouted at Mum, who was, of course, sat at the table in front of her laptop. (I think she might actually have lost the ability to walk!) Mum looked up at the yuck things and then at me and said, 'Darling, I didn't want to pry but I assumed you'd be starting your period very soon and I thought you'd need some of those so that you're not caught off guard.' I suddenly felt a bit bad that I was so cross with her, but I didn't really know what to do so I just kept going. (Man, it's hard to back down when you've started a strop!) 'All right, okay, thanks but not these. No one wears these, are you mad?!' I mean, I know it was nice of her to think about it but she should have asked me, not gone right ahead and bought things old ladies wear and then plopped them on my bed for the whole world to see! What if I'd come home with one of my mates?! Oh, my god, can you imagine?! Or, practically as bad, actually, no, defs worse, Luke had gone into my bedroom?! I feel sick just thinking about what could have happened. I knew I should have locked my door when I left this morning. Thing is, I don't usually lock it when I'm out, only when I'm in. Obvs I'm going to lock it when I go out from now on, but, honestly, what was Mum thinking?!

I'll tell you what she was thinking. I know because she told me and this is just SO typical and unbelievable of her. I said, 'a) It's none of your business and b) when I do . . . you know –' I didn't want to say it in the kitchen even though Gran and Luke were out – 'start that, I am obviously not going to use these –' I gave the, bleurgh, THINGS a good shake to show her how serious I was – 'I am not a hundred years old!' She replied, 'My darling girl –' she knows I hate it when she starts sentences like that. Why can't she just say my name?! – 'tampons are much, much more difficult to use than sanitary towels.' (Oh god, I wanted to puke.) 'So I really think you should try them.' I could not believe what she was saying. Literally, I totes could not believe it. I was so cross I stormed out but only after I'd thrown the packet of those THINGS on the table really hard.

I'm in my room now and you won't believe what's just happened. I have actually started my period! How weird is that? It's like that row and seeing those things made it happen. Spooky or what?! I used one of the tampons I'd bought. And it was NOT difficult, like Mum had tried to make out. It was really easy. I'd thought it might be fiddly and feel weird but it really didn't. Major phew. TBH I do feel a bit stressy and my tummy feels a bit, I don't know, a bit puffy but, you know, I don't feel like majorly different or anything, even though I am now OFFICIALLY (as Grace would say) A WOMAN! Hah, hah. Thank god I had already bought the tampons because otherwise I'd have had to go downstairs and get those things back and Mum would have seen and defs would have said 'Told you so'!

I wasn't talking to Mum during supper obvs, but I could see she was trying to catch my eye. Then, afterwards, as I was about to come upstairs Gran said, but as Basil, 'Kat, don't you have something you want to say to Tabitha?' That made me laugh because Gran knows Mum hates it when she pretends Basil can talk. Mum gave Gran a cross look and said, 'Yes, thank you, Basil,' really sarcastically, so even though she was saying Basil, making out she was actually replying to him, she looked at Gran to make it super clear she wasn't joining in with the whole pretending-Basil-can-talk-game. 'I'm sorry about earlier and leaving those . . . erm . . . things on your bed and also of course I will pay for tampons. I don't always get being a good mum right, but I am doing my best.' I felt bad when she said that. I so do not like feeling sorry for Mum. 'Yeah, all right, you're an okay mum,' I replied, laughing so that she'd know I was joking about being an 'okay mum'. Mum laughed back and then tried to hug me – big mistake – I dodged the hug and said, 'Don't push your luck,' and Mum did smile, which was a relief. Because sometimes when I won't hug or kiss her she puts on a revolting baby voice and says, 'Why won't you kiss your mummy? She loves you so much.' Which makes me want to puke. Not because I don't love Mum. Obvs I do, but a) I hate the stupid voice and b) I cannot bear it when she talks about herself as if she were a different person or in what Luke says is called the third person. Random because why third person? If she talks about herself as if she was another person shouldn't it be 'second person'? Am obvs not going to get Luke to explain it, though. As if. If I can help it, I never give him a chance to show off his brain-boxiness.

MUZZY

About to go to sleep, got Muzzy tucked up with me because I do feel a bit funny . . . I think it might be the whole period business. I don't know but it feels odd. Exciting in a way, but sort of a bit freaky too. It is a whole new thing, isn't it? I know this is going to sound really weird but it's like I've just suddenly stopped being a little girl. I know I wasn't one really, well, not any more, but it is strange thinking that I could now have a baby because of this. Because that's what they're for, isn't it? I don't think nature would make us have them for fun. I just sort of wish I'd had a bit more warning, you know, like more time to get used to the idea that this major change was going to happen and I could never go back . . . Don't know how that would work, though!

I've just realised I didn't tell Mum. I kind of forgot to because of having been cross about the THINGS. I will tell her but she had better swear she is not going to write about it in her blog. I will literally die if she does and it is exactly the sort of thing she would write about too, so I'll have to make her double, quadruple promise.

Ooh, at least this means I deffo won't have it (the period) when it's my party. Thank god.

SPRING TERM
WEEK 10 (FRIDAY)

BAD CHANGES

On my walk to school I noticed that the new café has actually opened now. Oh man, it looks so incredibly cool. And the woman running it waved at me again as I passed by. Is that a bit creepy or just ordinary everyday friendly? I hope it's just friendly, you know, and she's doing it because she's new to the area and probably needs to be super nice and come across as all hey-come-in-y because she wants everyone to buy coffee and stuff, I guess. She's quite young, about twenty-five or so, and really hip. She's got tattoos up both her arms that were so big I even noticed them through the window. I didn't go in, though, obvs. I might soon but I don't want to be the first customer ever. That'd be totes embarrassing. Anyway, I'll bet a hot chocolate, which would be the only drink I'd want, is going to be really expensive and there is no way Mum is going to give me extra pocket money so I can have a hot chocolate every day, or even now and again, on my way to school. As if. Even if she did, like for a one-time thing, she'd go on and on about how I had to realise the huge amount of calories that it had in it and how it'd make me fat and rot my teeth and, basics, how that one hot chocolate was going ruin my whole life. You know, pretty much like all adults seem to do – you caj mention something fun and yummy and treat-y and they spoil it by doing a major lecture on how bad and awful and disastrous it is for you.

Oh god, yeah, got yet another text from Dad (he so can't take a hint). It said 'Long time no speak, look forward to seeing you at the GCSE evening next week.' He still thinks he's coming! Ridic, plus, hello, not going to happen. I haven't worked out how I'm going to stop him but I have to, defs. He just can't be there.

So, during first break, on my way back from the toilets, Aly (see, not calling her Dark Aly any more) came up to me. I was relieved I was on my own because even though everyone knows I'm doing the project with her I still don't want to be with the others when she comes up because I know Emz and A'isha are going to be all eggy and tease me if I'm even just okay with her. It's all right for them. They got put together for the project. I didn't exactly choose to be with her, I got put with her, so, you know, they should just shut up. Anyhoo, she was carrying two clipboards with charts on them and gave me one. 'Okay, so across the top we've got to put the things, activities etc., and then down the sides we'll mark how many boys and girls do each thing. Geddit?' I didn't really get it but I didn't say so because I figured I'd work it out as we went along. 'Then when we've done this, we'll collate the data and from that we'll be able to work out if more girls or boys do some or all or none of the same things and, bingo, that's our project,' Aly said cheerily, like that was the most super-clear thing anyone had ever said in the world.

'Collate the data'? Hellooooo?! The only word in that sentence I know is 'the'! I didn't know what to say. I was really pleased Aly had worked the whole thing out and was on top of how we were going to do this but I was panicking a bit too. If she was going to carry on saying things like 'collate the data', then how was I going to keep up? Or worse, was Aly going to turn on me if I didn't start saying words like 'collate' and 'data' and do the project on her own? I wouldn't normally care. You know me, not exactly Swot of the Year, but Mr Proper has said it's an automatic week's detention for people who fail to hand it in and I am not doing a whole week of detention. I don't mind one day here or there because it's sort of cool but a whole week? That is just legit boredom on a plate. I nearly backed out of it on the spot but then Aly said, 'So, shall we start this lunch-time?'

Yikes, that means spending the lunch break with her for two whole weeks. That is a lifetime. What if my bezzies all forget about me or, even worse, suddenly think I'm bezzies with Aly? That is way too long not to be with them every single lunchtime, like we always are. That is so extra.

Aly obviously realised there was something up because before I managed to say anything she sort of blurted out, like she was really trying to make out that it wasn't that a big deal, 'Or we could just do the rest of this week. That'd be four days, including today, if that's okay with you?'

And then I felt really bad because she'd obviously realised I wasn't that keen to spend two whole weeks with her at lunchtime. I don't want to feel bad about Aly. It's not like she's one of my mates. Anyway, I'm sure four days is actually enough to get the info we need, so, you know it'll be fine. And I'll make sure from now she doesn't ever think I don't want to be with her. I mean, I know I don't, really, but I'm not going to be horrible to her and I'm not going to be all join-y-in with the others if they're eggy about me doing the project with her either.

So, anyway, at the beginning of lunch Aly and I met up again (and I didn't make excuses to my lot – I just did it!) and we worked out what the categories (her word for 'things') for our experiment should be – they are:

1. Sitting alone in the canteen and waiting for someone else to join you and if no one does then just staying alone.
2. Hanging out with a group in the playground even when it's not good weather.
3. Playing sport, any kind, for the whole lunch break.
4. Working in the library during breaks – even when it's not exams.
5. Helping someone who's in trouble in the playground or the corridors/whatever even if they don't ask for your help.
6. Smoking behind the bins.
7. Volunteering to do things that you don't actually have to do.

Even though we both came up with that list as soon as we'd finished it I turned to Aly and said, 'I can already so tell which ones boys are going to do most of and which ones girls will do most of. It's so obvious.' 'You never know, we'll have to see and it doesn't matter anyway because it's about proving science through observed behaviour and that's the project. The project is not to find something that will prove boys aren't as nice as girls, that'll just be the bonus result!' Aly replied, laughing. I did laugh too, because that is exactly what I was thinking! I have to admit I was a bit impressed too, she'd obviously thought about it a lot. Plus I'll bet no one else does a project as random as ours either.

On the way home with my lot A'isha and Emz started going on a bit straight away, asking me what Dark Aly was being like and saying stuff like they bet her idea for the project was all goth-y and stupid. I got a bit annoyed and said, 'Look, we're not going to call her Dark Aly any more, and if you must know her idea is really good,' and then I just said, 'See you tomorrow,' and walked off. I obvs don't want to fall out with them, and they're still my bezzies, but I don't want to have to be horrible about Aly all the time. I know I started all the calling-her-Dark-Aly stuff and I realise she's still a bit out there and extra and everything, but that doesn't mean I have to keep being mean about her all the time, does it? I'm not saying she's going to be my new best friend or anything major like that, I'm just, I don't know, I'm sort of interested in this project thing (I know, me?!) and it'll be easier to do and more fun if us lot give the whole Dark-Aly-she's-a-scary-sulky-goth thing a bit of a rest.

Later, back at home, just as I was about to take Basil and Scramble out for a walk Gran jumped up – well, jumped up as much as a granny can actually jump up – and said, 'Ooh, you might see Sam and I've knitted the most adorable thing for Kiki.' And then she whipped out the thing. Oh my actual god, you would not believe it, it is an actual dress, *an actual dress*. I repeat A DRESS FOR A DOG. Kill me now.

And I have got to give it to Sam. I have actually got to hand it over, all super caj, making out like people do this sort of thing every day: a knitted dress for his puppy to wear. I can't make a joke about it. I've literally got to say something like, 'Oh, yeah, here you go, it's a dress for Kiki. Hope she likes it!' Sam is going to think I am bonkers! If I didn't have a gran who knitted stuff for dogs I would defs think it was bonkers. I know Sam already knows what Gran's like and obvs he's seen Basil in his outfits but I'm actually going to be giving him one for his own dog. Aaargh. As I was leaving Gran said, but as Basil, 'I think my daughter is going to look very pretty in the dress Mummy's made her, don't you, Tab?' I looked at Gran and gave her a quick smile and then replied to Basil. 'Yes, well, let's see, maybe we won't see Sam and Bonnie and Kiki today.' That what was I was hoping. Gran being Gran replied, as Basil again, 'Not to worry, if we don't see them today, we can take the dress out again with us tomorrow and the next day and the next until we *do* see them. Kiki must get the dress after all the effort Mummy's made.' Grrr, I knew Gran was saying that to make me feel guilty!

So, of course, just my luck, I did see Sam and he had both dogs with him. It was really nice to see him and he looked totes gorge. When I handed him the dress, which, thank god, Gran had put in a bag, I said, 'It's from my gran for Kiki but please don't look at it while I'm here.' I did not think I could blag the whole super-caj thing in front of him. But he just said, 'No problem,' and stuffed it into his jacket pocket.

Sam is lovely. He's never annoying. He's just really nice all the time. Hmm, maybe I do sort of want him to be my boyfriend. How does that happen, though? How do you suddenly make someone your boyfriend instead of your friend? I can't exactly ask him, can I? And who makes the decision? Is it like a who-goes-first game? I wonder if there are, like, rules to follow, like an instruction book. I'm not a moron; I know there prob isn't an actual How To Make Someone Your Boyfriend book. But, you know what, that wouldn't be such a bad thing, would it? Because if you've never had a boyfriend, or, like me, turned a sort of friend into your boyfriend then a book that sort of helped you find out what you're supposed to do would be pretty useful, wouldn't it? Sam is my friend, isn't he? We don't exactly hang out but I think we're still friends, yeah? This is probably the sort of thing I should talk to Mum about because she had boyfriends before Dad and, bleurgh, she's got a boyfriend now. Hah, oldmanfriend, more like! I'll think about talking to Mum about it but, as usual, she will have to SWEAR ON HER LIFE not to write about it in her blog!

SPRING TERM
WEEK 11

(MONDAY)

TESTING TIMES

Oh god, I don't know what I'm going to do. I'm really upset but I'm cross too. This whole thing is so unfair. I can't believe it's happened either. It's all just blown up over nothing. I literally cannot believe this is happening. You know how usually all four us, my gang, my bezzies, Emz, A'isha, Grace and me, all meet up every day so we can walk into school? Well, today, Emz and A'isha didn't show up. They just weren't there. Grace was and we waited for a bit but we couldn't be late because school have got this ridic new thing that if you're even a tiny bit late they make you miss the whole first period, which, of course, then means they write a letter home saying you missed the first period like it was your fault you'd missed it in the first place! There was no text from either of them so I did wonder where they were and what was going on but I didn't think anything major had happened, just that maybe they were both late or something.

Huh, well, I was wrong, big time. As soon as I saw them at school – they were both together, like they'd planned it – they completely blanked me. They acted like I wasn't there. And they did that all day long! Even in the classes we do together. I was at our table, obvs – we always sit at the same table – and they made a really big deal of ignoring me. It was so embarrassing and obvious. Even Grace, in the classes she's in with us, realised what they were doing and made a 'what's going on?' face at me. It was horrible. I nearly cried I was so upset. I knew immediately it was all about me saying they shouldn't be mean about Dark Aly, which is just so ridic and stupid of them. Okay, maybe I shouldn't have stormed off yesterday but I don't think me doing that means I deserve to be frozen out of my own gang of bezzies. Now I'm really worried they won't come to my party either, and maybe they'll make the others not come too. It's only in just over a week. Oh god, I wish I wasn't having it now. I hate my stupid party and the stupid mocktails idea and I wish it wasn't happening. My two so-called-bezzies probably won't come and then no one else will and I'll just look like some loser with no mates and it'll be a disaster.

But the thing is, I don't think it should be me who tries to make it up. I didn't do anything. It's not like I said, 'Hey, guys, I prefer Aly to you lot now,' or anything ridic like that. And it's not like they spent all day every day being horrible to her either and I've made them stop doing that. None of us hardly paid her any attention. And it's not like I've said, 'Can she be in our gang?' I literally have not done one single thing to deserve this. I cannot believe they are freezing me out like this.

On the way home Grace was sweet and said I shouldn't panic and that they'd probably be back to normal tomorrow, but I'll bet they won't. I bet they never talk to me again. During lunch break when Aly and I were doing the checklist thing for our project I could see them – Emz and A'isha – over the other side of the canteen and I just knew they were talking about me. I am absolutely sure they were. Oh, it's all gone wrong but it is NOT my fault. I cannot believe how unfair they're being. I am not going to back down first, though. It's their problem, not mine. Obvs it is my problem because I'm so upset, but I'm going to try to act like I'm not that bothered and defs not let them see that this has got to me because that way it'll look like I'm in the wrong and I am not, am I?

WHATEVS

So, what's new? Right, because I am not going to think about YKW I am going to talk about the project. I was so right. It's defs mainly boys who do the things I said they'd do, like never stay sitting alone in the canteen. And it's defs mainly girls who do the things nicer people do, like talk to people who are in trouble and stuff like that. Knew it. Girls are nicer than boys, and more intelligent, interesting and kinder, legit. You've only got to look at me and Luke to know it's true – no brainer alert. Yes, all right, I guess he is brainier, if you count brains as being a swotty nerd pants, but then he's not like a regular boy-boy, you know what I mean? Actually, though, thinking about it, since the whole Poo In The Loo thing he is defs being a bit more boy-y, which is so random because normally he's just a standard geek with his head stuck in a book about the planets. I am sure he's got a poster up in his room of some pop-star girl – hilarious. And a bit disgusting too. I do not want to think about Luke getting crushes on girls – mankenstein or what? Yuck, it's making me feel sick just thinking about it. He is eleven now so, you know, maybe this is when boys start thinking about girls. How completely revolting. I know I think about Sam and stuff, but that's different and anyway I'm three years older than Luke so it's much more normal.

Oh yeah, at supper Luke said he'd got a letter from that Swots-And-Nerds-Only school he's going to in

September and apparently it said he was going to be paired up with an older boy from the school who lives nearest to us so that he could be 'mentored' by this other boy and also make the first few journeys with him. Big deal. No one paired me up with anyone from HAC. I don't see why Luke is so special he gets to be mentored, whatever that means. Mum was thrilled, of course. 'Oh, I'm so pleased. I was worried about you doing that long journey all alone. What a great scheme. How wonderful!' Dumbledore Chops was there, as per, and he gave Luke a sort of jokey punch on the shoulder. What an idiot! What was he trying to say with his supposedly funny punch? Hey, we're both guys together, mate?! I was pleased though, because even though everyone was being all 'Oooh, you're so marvellous, let's talk about everything to do with you' Luke gave me a quick grin and said, 'Ow, Frank, that hurt.' We both knew it didn't, though. It was hilarious because Dumbledore Chops looked really embarrassed and sort of grinned at Mum, who did an 'It's all right' face back at him. Puke. Obviously he can do no wrong. Gran knew we were mucking about, though, and gave me and Luke a bit of a 'stop that' look. I wonder if Gran thinks Dumbledore Chops is as utterly amazeballs in every way as Mum obviously does.

DUMBLEDORE CHOPS

← NOT A COOL BEARD

'What do you most want for your birthday, Tab?' Dumbledore Chops suddenly asked me, obvs trying to make everyone forget about his stupid punch. Random or what? We were not talking about my birthday; we were, as per, talking about Super Nerd Gnat Features Luke. Mum turned to look at me and so did Gran. I didn't know what to say. I mean, was I supposed to literally tell him what I wanted and he'd then go and buy it? Or was he just making conversation? (Boring.) Or was he asking me for Mum? I couldn't work it out so in the end I just said the truth: a laptop.

Mum, annoyingly, laughed out loud and then said, 'And in the real world what would you like?' So super irritating of her. I don't see why I shouldn't have a laptop. She's got one. I know she's a grown-up and writes a column and stuff but, still, I need a laptop. I bet I have much more homework to do than she has columns to write. And I'm sure I'd do my home-work much better if I had one. It's so unfair the way Mum gets to decide. 'Yeah, well, that's all I want,' I said and then left the table in a strop. And as if things weren't bad enough Luke went, 'Oooh, who's in a bad mood?' as I walked out. Idiot.

LUKE

I know I am actually in a bad mood and I know it's because of what's happened with Emz and A'isha. But I can't help it. And I can't stop thinking about it. They are two out of my three best friends. I've only got one now and what sort of loser has only one best friend? Two bezzies don't make a gang either. I loved being in a gang of best mates. And I suppose I am being a bit silly about wanting a laptop. I know they cost a fortune and it's not as if I don't know we haven't got any money. But it's not like no one in the world my age never gets laptops. Just not me, basics. So, no laptop and no gang. Huh, I feel really great. Not. My whole life has gone wrong and it's not even my fault.

SPRING TERM
WEEK 11

(TUESDAY)

A SORT OF TREAT

I **so didn't** want to go into school today. I was dreading more of the Emz-and-A'isha-not-talking-to-me treatment. I was so worried that I'd cry in front of them and that would just be so awful and incredibly embarrassing. I know Grace would be nice if I cried but I don't know what the other two would do, especially if they're not talking to me. They might just think: *Yeah, serves you right.* But they might feel bad and stop freezing me out. I don't know.

Because of all this I'd forgotten that there was a late start this morning. Amazingly Mum had remembered, only because she'd got a text. Remembering Proper Mother stuff like that is not what Mum does usually! Then, completely randomly, Mum said, 'There's a new café opened round the corner. Shall we go and check it out together before you go into school?' I couldn't believe it but, I admit, I was pleased. We went in and the woman who'd waved at me said, 'Oh hi, it's you, late start?' It was really nice and made me feel like I knew her, which obviously I actually don't, but you know. Mum replied, 'Yes, they never had them in my day.' And the woman said, 'They did in mine. I was at HAC too. I recognise the uniform, still crap, isn't it?' she said, looking at me, smiling. She didn't seem to think saying 'crap' in front of my mum was a big deal. I mean, I know it isn't really, but I don't think I'd say in front of a grown-up. She is so cool. I can't believe she went to my school. How fantastic is that? Mum ordered a coffee for her and a hot chocolate for me and, best of all, didn't say one word about how fattening it was or that it was a one-off treat or any of that boring stuff that would've spoiled it.

And then, I don't really know how it started, but it wasn't eggy or weird, Mum just started asking me stuff, not pushily or nosily or in a way that made me think she might use it in her column. I told her about starting my periods, which, thank god, she just nodded at, and didn't do a whole, 'Oh, my baby's become a woman' crazy thing or anything like that, which TBH I had really worried she might. And then we talked about that, not that there's much to say, but it was all so nice and I sort of ended up telling her about what's happened with Emz and A'isha and she was really good about that too. She didn't give me solutions or advice, which would have annoyed me. I hate it when you tell grown-ups something's wrong and they go straight into 'Right, what you have to do is this . . .' And you're thinking: *I don't want to know how you'd deal with this. It's my problem, and I just want to talk about it not get a lecture on how to fix it the way you would.* But she didn't do that at all. She just listened and then said, 'It must be very hard for you, darling. I hope things get back to normal soon.' Amazeballs.

She was so chilled. No lecture and no 'Well, here's where you were in the wrong' stuff either.

But we did have a bit of a row when she tried to explain why it was okay for Dad to come to the GCSE options eve. Mum kept saying it was his choice and that she couldn't stop him and how he behaved when he was there was also his choice, blah, blah, blah. Basics she was giving me all that 'we are separate people now so what Dad does is his call and I can't make him do anything' stuff, which is probs THE thing I most hate about them being split up. I just don't want to hear all that. I want Mum to make sure Dad doesn't turn up and embarrass me to death. I mean, that's what she used to do, before they split up. She'd always do all the things that were anything to do with school or other parents or whatever and Dad would stay at home or wherever he was and that way I never had to even think about whether he was drunk or wouldn't behave like a grown-up. But now Mum's basics telling me that I'm on my own with whatever he does because 'it's not her job' to control Dad. I suppose that's why they split up, because you never know when he's going to behave like a grown-up, but I do think it's a bit unfair that she won't stop him coming to my school. I'll bet she could if she really wanted to.

And then, just before we left, Mum asked me if I'd like to talk about Frank aka Dumbledore Chops! Majorly mankenstein. Can you believe it? No, thank you very much. As if. Why on earth would I want to talk about him?! She might think he's the most interesting thing in the whole wide world but I certainly don't. Yuck. I don't know what she had in mind, probably some 'How do you feel about him?' type of convo, but there is no way I'm doing that. Anyhoo I'm pretty sure Mum does not want to hear what I actually feel about him!

DUMBLEDORE
CHOPS

NOT A COOL
BEARD

It was nice to be alone with Mum, though. Defs better than having Big Poo In The Loo there. I can't remember the last time we did anything like that. In fact, I don't think we ever have. Defs not since we moved to Gran's, that's for sure. And Mum is definitely more, I don't know, sort of chilled, I guess, since we came to live with Gran.

It felt good to chat to Mum about Emz and A'isha not talking to me and she said I shouldn't worry about who's in the wrong or right, but just to work out how to make it all better. I know she was trying to help but that's easy for her to say! What I want is for us all to be the same again and for me to not feel horrible and be left out but for that to happen without me being the one who has to crawl back and beg their forgiveness. It's not that I can't say I'm sorry; it's that I can't, actually won't, say sorry when I haven't done anything wrong! Obvs I can say sorry to teachers and old people even when I know deep down inside I'm not in the wrong because otherwise they go on and on and on forever and never let it drop, so it's just easier to say sorry to get it over and done with in those situations. But this is completely different. I so don't deserve it and I would absolutely defs never ever do it to either of them. I know they were bezzies before I joined HAC but I do think it's super unfair of them to go straight back to being just the two of them, you know, how they were before I came along, just to punish me for something that wasn't even that big a deal.

Emz and A'isha were like it again at school. I knew they were going to be so I ignored them first sort of thing, so that they didn't have a chance to make me feel bad. I wasn't going to be all friendly if there was the remotest chance they were going to keep freezing me out, so at least I got in first with not talking to them, which might sound a bit stupid but it's better than trying to talk to them and then being ignored. Thinking about it now, though, I hope they hadn't decided to stop ignoring me and then re-decided to keep on when they saw I was ignoring them first. That couldn't have happened, could it? I mean, I'd have noticed it if they were about to stop ignoring me. Oh god, that would be the worst. I can't bear it if that's what happened. Please god, make that not be what happened today.

This is so horrible. It's the pits. I feel worse than I did when Mum and Dad split up. Much, much worse.

SPRING TERM WEEK 11

(WEDNESDAY)

DAD RUINS EVERYTHING - AGAIN

Well, there's nothing for it, tonight is the GCSE options eve and it looks like no matter what I say or do Dad is coming. Great. And Emz and A'isha completely ignored me at school again today, just like I knew they would. Double great. And if Dad does do something stupid it's not like I'll have them to be with. Hmm. At least we don't have to wear uniform when we go back to school tonight, which is something, I suppose. Anyway, I've decided I'm not going to sit around waiting for Emz and A'isha to realise that it's them, in fact, who are in the wrong. If they haven't stopped this by . . . I don't know, but really soon, then I'm going to forget about them and start my own new gang with Grace and Aly. Yes, I know I said I wasn't ever going to be bezzies with Aly but it's actually been quite fun doing this project with her and she can be really funny in a sort of you-don't-realise-she's-being-funny way. Like the other day we were on day four of our checking what girls and boys do differently outside of class and there was this boy sitting alone, so we were waiting for him to get up and join another group because, so far, we've worked out that boys never stay sitting alone for more than a few mins. Anyway, this boy did stay alone and then this girl from the year below us came and sat with him and Aly said, 'Ah, she must be in love with him,' and I said, 'No, that's her little brother. He's new.' And, get this, Aly said, completely straight-faced, 'So? Doesn't mean she doesn't luurve him.' I looked at her and said, 'Are you serious? How mank-enstein is that? Totes disgusting. Yuuuck.' And then Aly just looked back at me, not smiling. In fact, she was doing one of the faces she used to do, you know, all scary goth, and she replied, 'Well, Tabitha, you know, it does happen. I happen to be in love with my brother.' I am not joking. That is what she actually said. I really believed she was being completely serious and was all super-caj about brothers and sisters falling in love with each other, like it was normal and not that big a deal, plus telling me about her own actual brother. I thought I was going to be sick. And I didn't know what to say because I was actually thinking, *Oh my actual god, are you for real?* And in that moment I was really regretting ever having thought she was okay, but then she cracked up and said, 'Hah, got you! I haven't even got a brother!'

She so totes did get me. I really, really had believed, well, just for a bit, that she was being serious. I laughed out loud because it was pretty funny. It was such an out-there random thing to say anyone might have believed she meant it, especially because of how Aly has always been, all those in-your-face things she's said to teachers and being all gothy and stuff. How was I to know she was actually joking? She seemed so serious, so that's why it was so hilarious when she let on it was a joke. Though I admit until she let on she was winding me up I was a bit freaked out. So, she can be a laugh.

We've got to hand in our projects tomorrow and, TBH, I do think ours is pretty good. We've defs noticed major differences between boys and the girls (apart from the major, most obvious one that you do not need a project to notice, hah, hah!). I'm not absolutely sure what it all means but Aly reckons it's exactly what Mr Proper asked for – examples of science through behaviour, wasn't it? Or something like that anyway!

Got to go downstairs now, Mum and I are having early supper and then going to school for the GCSE thing. Apparently Dad's meeting us there. Kill me now. Literally.

SPRING TERM
WEEK 11 (WEDNESDAY)

LATER

Oh man, I don't know where to start. It's all so mixed up and crazy and so not how I thought it was going to be, but mainly in a good way, thank god! So, Dad wasn't drunk, big phew, but, sort of almost worse, he was being like I'd never ever seen him before, like on super best behaviour and sort of look-at-me-I-am-being-a-not-drunk-person-and-asking-a-whole-lot-of-questions-about-GCSEs. But like really over the top, like he was acting at being A Proper Dad. Like he'd read a How To Look Like A Proper Father at GCSE evenings. Random. And it was really weird. Even Mum raised her eyebrows at me when we stopped at the geography table and Dad straight away started asking about field trips! I couldn't say this in front of that teacher, but as if I am ever going to do geography GCSE, like, ever! But I couldn't get Dad to shut up and Miss Wigglesworth (I know, just how hilar is that name?!) was obvs so thrilled that someone was actually interested in her subject because I really don't think many people stopped at her table. Not even Grace is thinking about geography.

Us three went round all the tables, which teachers lay out like market stalls as if they're trying to get you to 'buy' their lovely things, i.e. the GCSE subject. Ridic or what? I knew Dad had no idea what he was doing when he actually stopped at the PE table and asked Mr Amir to, wait for it, 'Explain the academic element of a Physical Exercise GCSE.' I have no idea where Dad got this stuff from. Even Mr Amir, who is usually a bit shouty and grumpy (like most PE teachers!), looked like he was going to laugh at the question but he managed to keep it together, thank god. But then I noticed Emz and A'isha sort of hovering near the PE table and I just knew they were listening to Dad making a total idiot of himself with his bonkers questions about things like 'the relevancy of a PE GCSE in a workplace environment'.

I thought I was going to die of shame. Who asks a question like that?! I would almost have preferred it if Dad had been drunk! At least he doesn't do or say much when he's been drinking. I didn't dare catch either Emz or A'isha's eyes. I just knew they must be laughing at Dad and me. I probably would if I heard someone else's dad asking questions like that. Oh, it was awful. I just stood there and hoped the ground would open up and swallow me in. No such luck. Eventually, Mum, thank god, realised something was up and said, 'Well, I think we've seen enough for Tab to make her GCSE choices,' but in a voice that made it obvious, well, to me, anyway, that she was really saying enough was enough. But Dad obviously thought she was being rude and doing that thing grown-ups do of saying one thing but really meaning something else because he replied really loudly, shouting angrily, 'Well, I don't agree, we haven't finished looking round and I don't want to be told what to do by you of all people, thank you very much! And, for your information, I have not had a drink!!'

Oh, my god. I wanted to die. I literally thought I was going to pass out right there and then with embarrassment. The shame. Not only had he screamed his head off but he'd practically admitted he was an alky to the whole world. I had to try really hard not to burst into tears. I don't know what the matter was with him but I didn't care. All I could see was a million people – teachers, parents and basically the whole of my year – staring at him. I wanted to die right there and then. Mum hissed back at him, 'Keep your bloody voice down.' But Dad started shouting back at her, 'Why don't you keep your bloody voice down?!'

I couldn't take it. I just ran out of the hall and straight out of school. There was no way I was going to hang around and wait for them to have a full-on row in front of everyone. Mum tried to chase after me but I ran too fast. I ran all the way home.

I'm in my room now and I've locked the door. Mum's knocked loads of times but I am not going to answer. I'm so angry with her. I asked her to stop him coming and she should have done that. I knew he'd make a scene. I just knew he'd do something really, really embarrassing. I hate him. When I go into school tomorrow everyone is going to know that my dad is the shouty crazy alcoholic. Everyone is going to be looking at me and thinking about him being an alky who shouts at my mum, like one of those mad street drinkers. Like those guys who lie around on pavements waving stinky cans of lager and shouting random stuff at buses and passers-by. That is literally what Dad looked like. And I know Emz and A'isha saw it all too. That is just the cherry on the cake. Perfect. Brilliant. I wonder what else is going to go wrong now. Can't wait to find out. NOT.

SPRING TERM WEEK 11

(THURSDAY)

THE DAY AFTER MY LIFE ENDED

Obvs I left home as late as I could this morning to make sure I got to school just in time for the bell. You know, so that I didn't have to talk to or see anyone before class started. So that when I got there I'd just have to go straight to the classroom and not have time to be in the playground. But the absolute second I arrived I noticed straight away millions of my year staring at me — actually, no, not staring at me. They were all doing that thing when someone looks at you and then when you look back they look away really quickly because they don't want you to catch them looking at you. And you only ever do that when you've been talking about someone, don't you? Why would you look away? You wouldn't, you'd just smile or nod or do nothing if you didn't know them. You definitely would not snap your head back, desperately trying to make sure you didn't catch their eye. But that is exactly what everyone was doing. So I immediately knew that my whole entire year knew about what had happened last night. I was so upset I nearly turned round and walked straight out of school. I didn't care if I got into trouble. I just couldn't face everyone whispering and gossiping about me and my crazy dad. But then Aly burst in, obviously panicking she was going to be late, ran past me and said, 'Come on, let's knock everyone out with our brilliant project.' And I know it sounds weird, because we're not really proper mates but it did feel way better being able to go into class with someone and not have to skulk in looking at the ground to avoid everyone's eyes.

Anyway, just as I was about to sit down at Aly's

table – there was space obvs because she always makes a big deal about sitting on her own – I saw Emz and A'isha both beckoning me over. I was so completely thrilled and I was just about to go over when I suddenly thought, *No, wait a minute, you blank me for days and don't care that I'm really miserable and now you want me to dump Aly and come running back to you? Well, I'm not going to.* So, I just waved back at them super caj and sat down with Aly. Oh my god, you should have seen the look on their faces! Going by their expressions of total amazement I reckon they could not believe that I'd actually chosen to sit with Aly when they were happy to make up. I know Aly's a bit weird, plus the whole goth thing she's got going on, but she's been brilliant and a real laugh with the project and not been sulky and grunty at all. During the class I did start worrying I'd blown my chance to make up with Emz and A'isha and that maybe that had been the only go they were going to give me at being bezzies again, but I was also thinking that it was pretty cool of me not to have jumped back the absolute second they asked.

Anyhoo, at the end of class they both came up and A'isha said really nicely, 'Tab, we just wanted to say, both of us, that we're sorry about what happened last night with your dad and stuff. It must have been awful. We wanted to see if you're all right?' I was so pleased. SO, SO pleased. Before I had a chance to say anything, Emz said, 'Sit with us in the next class, yeah?' and gave me a huge everything's-okay smile. I felt really sort of split because obvs I desperately wanted to sit with my bezzies again and have it all like it was before but I also felt I couldn't suddenly go 'see ya' to Aly. For a split second I considered it but I could just feel Aly worrying that that was exactly what I was going to do. So I replied, 'Yeah, no probs, but Aly's going to sit with us too, though, right?' and then I gave Emz and then A'isha each a sort of 'that's the deal' stare, not like super stroppy but defs letting them know I really meant it.

Emz and A'isha looked at each other really quickly, even though it felt like ages – defs enough time for me to start worrying they were going to say 'nah, forget it' but they didn't. They both, at the same time, said, 'Yeah, sure.' And that was it. We all four sat together for the rest of the day, plus Grace when she was in our classes and it was BRILLIANT! Aly didn't do any sort of goth-y weird things. She was just like us mainly. And at lunchtime she was with us too. It just sort of happened and no one said anything and it was fine.

FRIENDS

Actually, during lunch break, Aly asked me in a really quiet and serious voice, 'Tab, so, is your dad an alcoholic?' Everyone turned to look at me. And then they looked at Aly and then back at me. I could tell no one knew what to say or think. And for a minute I didn't know what to say or do either, but then I decided I might as well tell the truth. 'Yeah, I guess, that's sort of why my parents split up.' And then, you will not believe this, Aly said, 'Yeah, mine too, except it was my mum. She's dead now, that's why I had to move schools and come here.' She said it in a really ordinary voice, not like she was trying not to cry or anything, just like she was telling us something pretty normal. All four of us looked at each other. No one knew what to say and we were all silent for a bit.

Then, and I know this is a bit random and I defs know it doesn't make up for your mum being dead, I just said, 'Do you want to come to my birthday party? It's mocktails?' There was a silence for a moment and I knew everyone was wondering if Aly was going to say something horrible and grumpy. 'Is that a party where we all take the mick out of cocktails?' said Aly. What? No one knew what she was talking about and then Grace, of course, got it first and burst out laughing. But the rest of us didn't. Aly looked at us all and said, 'Mocktails? Mock tails? A party where you mock the cocktails, geddit?' And then we all started laughing because that was funny, and clever. She can be a right laugh, it turns out.

On the way home I practically started skipping I was so happy. I'd got my bezzies back, and I'd done what Gran would call 'the right thing' with Aly and not dumped her. (I was especially pleased about that when we found out why she'd not been so very nice. I mean, can you imagine if I'd just gone back to my bezzies and forgotten about her and then found out about her mum?! I'd have died of shame.) And then, get this, it is the best thing ever, like ever, ever, ever! I walked past the new coffee shop and the girl who runs it, the one with the tattoos, was putting up a sign in the window when she saw me and popped her head out and said, 'Hey, maybe I don't need to put the sign up. Do you fancy working here for a couple of hours on Saturdays?' Can you actually believe it?! I was like, 'Yes, please!' straight away. This is just so totes BRILLIANT! I cannot believe my luck.

Her name is Rachel but she told me to call her CG. She said that's what everyone calls her. It's short for Coffee Girl because she's always been totes obsessed with coffee. How amazingly cool is that? I'm going to do four hours on Saturday from ten till two, which she said is her busiest time and she's going to pay me, £5 an hour! £5 an hour! That's £20 every Saturday. So, if you add that to my allowance, I'll be getting nearly £25 a week. This is just so amazeballs brilliant. I am so happy it is ridic!

I was in bed but I've got up to write this last bit – do you know what? The funny thing is, even though it was the worst thing ever and the most embarrassing, if Dad hadn't done what he did then Emz and A'isha might not have made it up with me, because they felt so sorry for me that they forgot about whatever they were cross about before. So, in a way, what he did was almost like a good thing! Random or what? Plus, and I've only just thought of this, Dad making his problem so obvious to everyone meant that Aly could tell us all about her mum's drinking. So actually Dad sort of did me a favour, although that is NOT what it felt like and I defs won't ever be thanking him for it or anything like that!

Oh my actual god. You are not going to believe this. It is officially An Actual Fact, and completely unbelievable, seeing as it's me. So, yesterday we gave our projects in and today Mr Proper said in class that of all the projects he'd had handed in he'd got one that was 'a perfect example of the sort of everyday anthropology I was looking for', and it was mine and Aly's! Mr Proper was talking about our project! Obvs I had no idea what 'anthropology' meant, especially because that is not what he'd called the project in the first place, but Grace and Aly explained that anthro-doo-dah is the actual word for 'observing human behaviour' and that this is what our project was supposed to be about. He then went on about how this project gave 'excellent yet accessible examples' (I am quoting here!) of everyday life at school, yet could just as easily have been observations from any adult workplace'! I know! He was super impressed. Amazeballs. And, wait for it, he said he was going to make the whole class read this project's 'findings' so that they all could challenge (that's 'think about' apparently) the choices they make from now on outside of class. BTW basics 'findings' means the things we wrote down about how many boys do this and girls do that etc. etc. So 'findings' is the posh word for results.

The whole time he was going on about the project he didn't let on that it was mine and Aly's he was talking about, which sort of made it all the more brilliant. He kept looking at us, like we were in on it, which obvs we were. So then, when he stopped raving about it, he paused, looked around, making out that he couldn't remember who'd done the project and then stretched his hand out towards Aly and me and asked us to come up to the front to take a bow – I am not joking! The whole class looked totes shocked and like they could not believe it was ours! Obviously no one had ever thought for one single minute that this 'excellent project' could have been done by us two! It was hilarious. We both did really huge bows, making a joke out of it all, but it did feel pretty fantastic. This is the first time in my life I've got this much approval from a teacher, legit.

Everyone clapped and whooped. It was absolutely fantastic! And no one made any 'what are you playing at?' faces at us either because, do you know what, I don't think anyone thinks I've suddenly turned into A Major Nerd or anything super un-cool like that. That's because the project was like A Thing. It's not like I've started asking for more homework or to help clear up the staffroom or anything ridic extra like that, is it? Anyway, because I did the project with Aly there wasn't that much danger of looking like I'd gone all Perfect Prefect because whatever she is she is not like that!

And then, when class was ending and everyone was jostling their way out of the door – the boys, as per, trying to squeeze through all at the same time together (we should have put that in our project because the girls never do that!) – Mr Proper asked Aly and me to stay behind for a minute because he 'wanted a word'. At first I thought, *Oh great, he's going to have a go about our spelling being rubbish or the font being too small or something random and boring like that*, because, you know, he's not called Mr Proper for nothing! He's always on at someone about how they didn't start a sentence with a capital or a comma was in the wrong place – tiny stuff that no one except him really cares about! But that was not what he wanted to talk to us about, thank god! Exactly the opposite, actually – he wanted, wait for it, to ask if Aly and me would start a club! A weekly debating club. I know! He said he thought the stuff we'd done in our project would be the perfect topic to start it off and that he reckoned both boys and girls would defs want to come because they'd get to argue about the differences between them. He's right, though, isn't he? Debating is actually just a posh word for arguing! He also said, 'No offence, but also if it's you two running the club then the cool kids won't think it's a nerds' thing,' and then he laughed and Aly and I starting laughing too. How more officially cool can you get than a teacher saying to your face that you are one of the cool kids?! Usually I get 'Tabitha Baird, you are disruptive this or annoying that or deliberately distracting others, blah, blah, blah.' But *this* is so exciting!

I know it's a bit of an un-me thing to do, but if you think about it, it isn't really, except, I suppose, the bit about us running the club, which is a little bit swotty, I guess, but I don't care. I just love it. Aly and me are going to be in charge of an actual club. And we're going to get to talk about things that are actually interesting to all of us in our year. And Mr Proper said he'd arrange for us to have juice and biscuits and I said, 'Well, in that case, everyone's going to come,' and he laughed.

I know A'isha, Emz and Grace will definitely come. I told them about it on the way home (we've gone straight back into doing that again, yay!) and then

A'isha yelled in a super-excited way, 'Oh man, this is just great. Once we've done the stuff from your project which, BTW, was brilliant, we can do one about Muslim girls and the hijab and all that. I cannot wait to see some of those Muslim boys trying to explain why we've got to wear it but they don't have to go to prayers!' And then we all started coming up with ideas for different weeks – it was fantastic.

I was still thinking about it and still super excited when I got in so I actually told Mum and Gran straight away and they were so pleased. It was quite sweet, because it's not like I came home with all A*s or anything major like that. It is just a club. But they were dancing about like I'd been made head girl or something, so, of course, Basil and Scramble starting dancing about too. And Scramble started doing his new thing of going round and round like he's trying to eat his tail. It is so hilar.

Oh yeah and when I took them out for a walk (the dogs, not Gran and Mum, hah, hah!) I saw Sam and that was really nice too. We ended up walking all our dogs together for a bit and it wasn't eggy at all, just sort of easy, even though every time I see him now I am thinking, *Are we going to be girlfriend and boyf?* Except this time I was thinking, *Is he going to mention the dress Gran knitted for Kiki?* because she wasn't wearing it. Actually you probably wouldn't take Kiki for a walk in that dress because it is more like a super-dressed-up dress. It's not really for regular caj walks. Hah, hah. That is assuming, of course, you think ANY dress on a dog is okay! But I was worrying that he and his mum had seen it and thought it was knitted by a crazy lady. I know Gran is a bit crazy – she'd have to be. I mean, who else knits outfits for dogs? But she's not crazy-crazy. Anyhoo, he didn't mention it but then at the very last minute, after we'd said goodbye and we'd turned to go our different ways, he called after me. 'You know that, erm, aah, thing your gran knitted for Kiki? It's a . . . a . . . dress, right?' What?! I couldn't tell if he was saying it in a 'Is she nuts?' way or in a 'Hey, it's cool, just checking' way. I didn't know what to say because actually I was a bit annoyed because, derr, OF COURSE it's a dress!

And him asking me that felt a bit embarrassing and a bit like maybe he was trying to get me to go 'Yeah, I know, crazy or what?' and then sort of laugh with him at Gran for making it. In the end I think I sounded a bit cross because I sort of blurted out, 'Yeah, thanks, I *do* know it's a dress,' and then I walked off. Aargh, I don't know why I did that. I was worried that he might be taking the mick but now I don't think he was and I'm sure I sounded really rude and he'll probs never talk to me because I'm so stroppy and unpleasant (more things teachers say to me).

I'll bet I've totes blown it with Sam. Assuming there was anything to blow! Oh god, I didn't mean to sound so narked, I was just trying not to sound like I thought there was anything wrong with what Gran had knitted. Obvs is it a bit embarrassing, but I can't let on because that feels like ganging up on Gran. But I had such a nice time with Sam and now he's probably gone completely off me because I was snippy. I'll bet I never ever see him again. Grrr, I hate knitting.

So, **today was** my birthday, well, it still is actually, but it's nearly not because it's almost midnight so then it won't be my birthday any more. Boo. It wasn't my mocktail birthday party day, that's next week. But I have had a great day! When I got the job at the café I hadn't realised that my first day there would be today on my actual birthday. And usually you'd probably think, *Rats, poo, boo — I have to work on my birthday*, wouldn't you? Except it was really brilliant.

I LOVE working there. It is soooo hip. Everybody who came in is like a super hipster. They all look like Rachel aka CG, with tattoos all over the place. And everyone was so nice and friendly to me. It's always majorly busy on Saturdays, CG said, and it defs was today – I didn't sit down once. My jobs are to take away cups and plates when people have finished (derr, obvs not *before* they've finished!), wipe the tables down and put papers and stuff away. CG has all the Saturday papers in a big wooden crate so that everyone can read them while they're there if they like. It is sooo chilled. It wasn't incredibly hard work but it was really busy and I had to wash up a bit too, because she hasn't got a dishwasher and there ended up being so many people we ran out of cups but I didn't mind that because it was all so fun. I'd better make sure Mum doesn't find out I didn't mind washing up!

When I came home Mum and Gran had done a special all-laid-out-on-the-table tea with smoked salmon sandwiches (my absolute fav in the whole wide world), crisps and nuts (and Mum didn't say anything when I ate them, result!) and a really delish chocolate cake with a chocolate cream middle Gran had made. It was a surprise. They hadn't told me they were going to do it. Just as well I came home after work, eh?! But I was a bit annoyed at first because Dumbledore Chops was there, shouting 'surprise!' with everyone like that was completely normal. You know, like why wouldn't he be here with my mum, little brother and gran for my surprise tea? I didn't think he should be at *my* birthday tea. He's not part of our actual family. But he was okay in the end and didn't do any 'howya doin?' embarrassing, I'm-so-down-with-the-kids trying-to-talk-to-me. And, guess what, he gave me a laptop! My very own laptop. It's not a new one. It's his old one, he said, but it's not scratched or super old or really slow or anything. I was so surprised because I am never that nice to him.

'I remembered you saying you'd like a laptop, so there you go. I hope it'll do until you can have a swanky new one,' he said a bit shyly as he handed it over. Mum was so pleased with him she gave him a huge kiss after I'd opened it. Yuck. But I admit it was really nice of him to give it to me because I don't think he was going to get rid of it. I think he's actually given me something he could still have used. But that does not mean Mum should kiss him in front of us. Ever. No, thank you. Major mankenstein. No parents, actually make that no old people, should ever kiss in front of their kids. It should be against the law and I am not joking. No one wants to see that. No one. Bleurgh. But apart from that I am VERY pleased with the laptop.

And Mum gave me quite a cool prez – she'd opened a bank account for me. It's all mine. I don't need her signature or anything AND she'd put £50 in it. Not bad, eh? It feels soooo grown up but in a good way. It's got a bank card with it, with my name printed on it (love that!) and I can get cash out with it and use it in shops to pay for stuff up to £20 max. There's so much more you can do just by turning fourteen. It's weird but GREAT.

Luke gave me a book token. Fantastic. Not. I reckon that was his idea of a joke. I know I am actually reading more and secretly loving all the books I've been reading but no one else knows. Defs not Luke, so I'm sure he gave me the book token in a sarky way, you know, to do a whole big look-here's-a-present-you-won't-want-but-*should* type of way. He couldn't know I now like reading because I'm still letting Mum believe I hate it because she'll only go on and on about it if she finds out. PLUS every time she sees me doing something that isn't reading she'll probs say, 'Now that you love reading, shouldn't you be reading a book, darling?' or something that'll annoy me and just make me go off reading again. I suppose I'm being a bit mean, the token was for £10 and he did buy it himself. But seeing as he doesn't actually get pocket money yet in a way it's not really his own money because Mum must have bought it for him. Okay, I guess that's a bit horrid of me and there is a new book I want . . .

Gran's present is totes random but I think I like it, still not completely sure, though. It's a crocheted dress made with gold thread. It is very fancy and defs a dress for when you're properly dressing up. 'That's for you to wear at your mocktail party,' Gran said when she gave it to me. It is really, really beautiful. I know technically it's knitted (if crocheting is a kind of knitting) but it doesn't look knitted. I think that's partly because it's not wool. It's sort of thick metally cotton. It is really pretty and I think I look all right in it. Actually more than all right, I think it looks good on me. It's got a scalloped hem, you know, when the edge isn't straight, it's like a whole line of half-circles instead. And Gran lined it with some gorgeous silky stuff too so you can't see between the crocheted bits, which if you could have done would obvs have meant I was never going to wear it! As if. I know celebs wear see-through dresses where you can see all their bits but I am never going to do that. Totes yuck, plus it's not a very good way to go around if you ever want people to take you seriously, is it? Anyway, I am mainly really pleased with the dress. The only thing is because it's homemade and really unusual and unique it feels a bit more look-at-me-y than a bought dress. Does that make sense? I do love it, I just don't want to be all look-at-me-I've-had-A-Special-Thing-made-Especially-For-My-Party. I know that is what Gran's done but I'm not sure that's what I want to be like.

I don't want to ask my bezzies what they think because then if I do wear it they'll be all 'Is that the dress you were worried about?' or it'll just bring extra attention to the dress and that is exactly what I don't want to do. I know, I can ask CG when I'm working next Saturday before my party. I'll take the dress in and see what she thinks. She'll defs know what to do cos she's so cool.

Got a birthday card from Dad, which was actually quite funny. He said he was really sorry about the GCSE night and wrote 'Your teachers said I must do better', which made me smile. He also asked if he could come up and take me out for supper soon 'now that you're so grown up'. I will probs say yes to that. It'd be cool to go out to a proper restaurant. We never go out cos Mum says she can't afford it. And I'm pretty sure Dad won't drink, at least on that night, because he's obvs really sorry about how badly the other night went. Thank god.

So, I reckon I've had a pretty good birthday. And I've still got my party to come, yay! Didn't get anything from Sam. Not that he knows it's my birthday or anything. Just saying. Haven't seen him since I sort of shouted at him. It's defs over. Uh, not that it had even started. Thinking about it, I didn't really shout-shout at him, I was a bit annoyed, so, you know, it wasn't like I made a big huge scene or anything . . .

I thought Mum was going to have a go at me about taking the café job without talking to her first about it but, amazeballs, when I told her (and I did tell her – I didn't ask permish!) she said she thought it was 'really independent and admirable' of me! Random. I was sure she'd say it was going to interrupt my GCSEs and I'd never get good grades if I was working too, blah, blah, blah. But she didn't. Coolio Julio.

Oh yeah, Luke got a letter from his Nerds-Only School with a date for him and Mum to come in to meet his mentor-match who will 'accompany' him to school. All sounds a bit much to get to school. I mean, it's not like he's doing the Olympics or climbing a huge mountain — he's just going to a school that isn't that near our house. Big Deal.

EASTER HOLIDAYS WEEK 1

(FRIDAY)

GRAN BECOMES ALAN SUGAR (SORT OF)

Oh yeah, get this, I passed CG's café the other day when I was walking Basil and Scramble. It's not my usual way, but I don't want to bump into Sam right now because if he has gone off me then it's going to be super awks and if he hasn't how am I going to know that he hasn't? I mean, how would I be able to tell? Because, if you think about it, if he's all normal it won't defs mean he isn't annoyed with me for before, will it?

The only way I'm going to know for sure he isn't cross with me will be if he gets in touch. You know, sends a text or something, and he hasn't done that, so . . . And anyway Gran had put Basil and Scramble into her latest creations of matching jackets and hats. Oh my god, you should see them. It is actually the most hilar thing I have ever seen in my life. Even more hilar than the coatigan Gran made before. If I didn't have to walk them in this gear I would be laughing my head off. They are like men's suit jackets with long sleeves and buttons down the front, except because Basil and Scramble are dogs and walk on all fours the buttons do up underneath them. If they were the sort of dogs who could stand up then they would SO look like they were wearing miniature suits, except, thank god, Gran has not made matching trousers. Even Gran isn't crazy to knit actual trousers for her dogs – each pair would have to have four legs for starters! And where would they do up?!

'It's a bit chilly out, Mummy, so I'm very pleased to have my nice new warm jacket and so is my little boy too,' Gran said to herself in Basil's voice. Obvs 'little boy' was what Basil meant – hah, hah, sorry, *Gran was pretending* Basil meant – for Scramble. Mum was sitting at her computer, as per, on the other side of the room but she heard and said, but without looking over, 'Mummy—' saying it exactly the way Gran had said it, although she never calls Gran 'Mummy', it's always 'Mum' – 'I am a dog so I cannot speak, therefore could you please stop doing that irritating voice for me and putting words into my mouth?'

Gran, without looking back at Mum, replied, but as Basil, 'I know, Mummy, I think my big sister is jealous of my smart new jacket. Maybe you should knit one for her too?'

I knew this would drive Mum mad and it did. She stood up and shouted at Gran, 'For the love of god, Mum, if you must pretend your stupid dog has a voice at least stop referring to him as my bloody brother!!!!' I thought I was going to wet myself I was laughing so hard. For once I so wished Luke was there. Those two are even worse than me and him. It is hysterical and I know Gran does it mainly to annoy Mum, which I admit is pretty babyish of her, but then Mum shouldn't let Gran wind her up like that. If Gran wants to pretend her dog is her son and he can speak, then who cares really? Gran gave Mum a sickly smile, which I just knew meant she was going to keep going, and said, 'Oh dear, Mummy, my big sister is getting in a flap, isn't she? Shall I go over and give her a kiss to make it all better?' Again, this is as Basil. Gran knew Mum would know that she meant Basil was going to kiss her! That did it. Mum screamed, 'For crying out loud, Mum, you are completely off your rocker. If you carry on like this I am going to put you in a home!' Then she stormed out of the room. I could not stop laughing, but I did feel a bit mean because Gran shouldn't really be like that to Mum, she is her mum – she's meant to be more grown up than her! Not that that's how it works. Sometimes Mum is much less grown up than me. It's true! Spesh when she's with YKW. Yuck.

So, when I walked past the café CG spotted me with the dogs in their 'snazzy' (Gran's word) outfits and came rushing out. 'Oh my god, those dogs are just too cute. I love what they're wearing, did you make them?' Hellooo?! I wanted to reply: Knit? Me? As if. Are you having a laugh? But I don't know her that well yet so I said, 'No, my gran knits lots of different things for them to wear. That's her, erm, thing. She's really good at knitting.' 'Well, they are amazing, fantastic, just brilliant,' CG went on, kneeling down and tickling Basil all over, which he, of course, lapped up because, as Gran keeps saying, in 'his voice', 'I do love the ladeeez.' Puke. After a bit I said I'd better get on with walking them and as I left CG said, 'You know, I know loads of people who'd buy custom-made outfits for their dogs if there was a place they could get them. Ask your gran if she'd be interested in doing that . . . you know, for money.' And then CG took a picture with her phone. 'I'm going to show my dog-loving mates; they are going to love this stuff.'

I can't believe there are other people in the world who actually want knitted stuff for their dogs! And I defs can't believe there are super-hip types, like all CG's mates must be, who'd like it! I thought Gran was the only person on the planet who thinks it's normal and okay. It's not like you ever see other dogs in jaunty knitted things, is it? And you never see that sort of get-up in pet shops, do you?! Okay, some people put felt jackets and waistcoaty things on their dogs when it's really cold but no one puts them in sweaters, coatigans, bonnets and floppy hats! Never mind the 'dress' she's knitted for Kiki! Can CG be right? Would people buy Gran's stuff if only they knew where to get it?! I hope she wasn't joking. I don't think she'd do that. You know, take the mick like that. She must be serious. Wow. I'm sure Gran would absolutely love to knit for more dogs. Oh man, that would be her idea of heaven on toast! And she'd earn a bit of money, which she's always saying we need. Hey, if there really are people out there who actually do want that stuff, she might end up earning loads. Gran could start a website and sell all over the world. It could be called something like . . . I dunno . . . Dog Knits? Nah, that sounds like the dogs have got lice. Or Fluffy Dogs? Eurgh, that's a bit creepy. Ooh, what about Woollies for Woofies? That's quite good, isn't it? Woollies for Woofies — for all your doggy's knitted needs. Pretty good, huh?

I didn't mention it to Gran until just now, after supper, when I was sure we'd be alone. I didn't want Mum around. After their fight earlier I thought she might grab the chance to tell Gran she was nuts and that no one would buy her stuff etc. etc. So when Mum had gone out to see her spesh boyf as per, yuck, and Luke was having a bath, I told Gran all about it. She got so excited. 'Ooh, my two favourite things, apart from you and Luke, of course — dogs and knitting! You can tell your boss I'm on!' And when I told her we could start a website and call it Woollies for Woofies she started jigging about with excitement, like she does, and Basil and Scramble joined in. It was very funny. Because no one else was there and it was just Gran and me I danced about a bit too, to join in and because it is a great laugh if no one is looking.

Best of all is that Gran is just soooo pleased and excited about it and has already come up with a million different outfit ideas. Some of them are a bit, erm, out there, like a cowboy's outfit for when someone's dog gets invited to a fancy-dress party??!! Helloooo. I don't want this whole thing to get totes ridic. I mean, does anyone have a party for their dog? And if they do, do they have fancy-dress ones?! I think I'll have to calm Gran down and suggest that she starts with doing just her usual coats and hats before she offers them that kind of stuff. Hah, hah, get me: 'usual coats and hats'?! Like they are normal! Do you know what, though? Thinking about it, they actually *are* normal if you compare them to things like a cowboy's outfit!

MY MOCKTAIL PARTY IS TOMORROW – I AM SOOOOOOO EXCITED!!!

EASTER HOLIDAYS
WEEK 1

(SUNDAY)

PARTY ON DOWN LIKE IT'S MY BIRTHDAY (PARTY!) BECAUSE IT IS!

OMG, OMG, OMG, OMG – OH, MY AAAACTUUUUAL GOD! Last night was my party, my mocktail party, and it was just the BEST EVER!!!!! It was completely brilliant in every single way and amazing and soooo much fun – everyone said they had The Best Time! I am soooo pleased.

So, I did wear the dress Gran had made me. I just decided to go for it. Plus I sort of had to — Mum had bought some super-gorge gold pumps to match, as an 'extra present', she said, which was really nice of her because I didn't ask for them or anything. But she gave them to me in front of Gran, saying, 'I couldn't resist getting you these because they will be just perfect with your dress.' My first reaction (but I didn't say it out loud) was: yeah, great, I can hardly admit now that I'm not sure about the dress! But in a way it was good because it meant I had no choice. There was nothing for it. I was going to have to wear the dress. And I am SO glad I did. The pumps were defs the sort of finisher — you know how you can be not sure of something you're wearing and then when you put it with something else it's, like, hello, bingo?! Well, that's what it was like with the pumps; the dress was made totes perfect by them. I wore black tights and my big gold hoops. I'd raced back from work (ooh, look at me 'raced back from work'?! I sound like some swanky lawyer or something!) to get everything set up for the party. I was panicking a bit because I didn't have that much time and I'd only organised a few bits in advance, like fruit juices to make the cocktails. But when I got back I nearly died because there was only about an hour left before the party started and Dumbledore Chops was there in the kitchen with mess all around him. I thought he was making supper or something super annoying five minutes before my party. I was just about to have a major go at Mum except it turned out all the mess was Dumbledore Chops getting the mocktails ready because he's an ace cocktail maker! Mum had asked him to come over and make them for my party as a surprise.

Oh man, it was brilliant. He brought loads of coloured jugs and paper umbrellas and fantastic crazy shaped straws and plastic sticks with tinsel on the end and cherries and pineapple and just every single thing you could ever think of putting in a cocktail, and some you wouldn't like tiny plastic animals and miniature palm trees. It was totes hilar.

Dumbledore Chops was getting so into it, shaking the cocktail shaker above his head and dancing around our tiny kitchen and I suddenly got a bit panicky that he and Mum might try to join in but they didn't, thank god. They all, Gran and Luke too, went out and took Basil and Scramble with them. I wouldn't have minded those two staying because everyone thinks they're adorable, but they might have got a bit excited and weed everywhere right in the middle of my sophisticated mocktail party. And even if they're cute, a dog weeing at your party is not a good look.

Dumbledore Chops – okay, I'm going to call him by his proper name now because he was so amazeballs. So, Frank made four huge jugs of mocktails. One of them even had a bunch of sparklers sticking out of the top – it all looked FANTASTIC. Mum and Gran had really tidied up the kitchen/living room (a first!) and pushed the table up against one wall so the space looked much bigger. And they'd covered the table in a really colourful plastic tablecloth and laid out a whole bunch of the sort of snacks you have at a cocktail party – mini sausages, little blocks of cut-up cheese on skewers with pineapple chunks (what a revolting combi I thought, but Mum says everyone used to have them at cocktail parties), olives with little bits of red peppers inside them (bleurgh, but I know at least Grace totes loves olives), crisps, salty nuts and a whole mound of teeny baby sandwiches. And, on top of all that, Frank had brought proper cocktail glasses – you know, those ones that look like an upside down pyramid and each one was a different colour with a long coloured stem. They looked so sophisticated and properly cocktail-y. He laid them out in a row, in front of the jugs full of mocktails, all ready to have the drinks poured in – it was just brilliant. I was soooo happy.

As they were leaving, before my bezzies turned up (I'd made them all promise to be a bit early so they'd be to be the first to arrive and I wouldn't be waiting on my own feeling all super eggy), Mum gave me a big hug (well, okay, I let her!) and said, 'Fact — when a party is properly prepared it always goes well, enjoy!' And she was right. It went totes brilliantly. Better than I'd ever thought it would and I know that was partly because of the amazeballs mocktails. Everyone loved them and the food and the whole thing. And every single one of my mates, even Aly, wore proper cocktail dresses. All right, Aly's was a teensy bit more goth-y than cocktail-y. It was black, of course, with long sleeves, but at least it was a dress and she said she hadn't worn a dress since nursery so it was really nice of her to make the effort I thought.

And we all danced. It was GREAT. I'd done a play-list, so it was like non-stop music the whole time and we all danced together in one big bunch. It was totes hilar! I had THE best time ever, deffo! And then, in the middle of the party, this is so amazing, I got a picture text from . . . yes, Sam! You will never ever guess what it was – it was sooooo cute – Kiki in her dress! She looked soooo adorable in it too, not crazy or weird, just super-super adorable. I showed it to everyone and they were all like 'aaaw' and 'OMG, did your granny knit that?' and A'isha, of course, was all, 'Never mind the dress. He soooo fancies you,' which was super embarrassing, although obvs I'm pleased that was what she thought too, natch. Even I think sending me that pic is quite . . . I dunno . . . I-defs-like-you-y, don't you? It's pretty flirty, isn't it? I mean, if you didn't *like* like someone you'd never send them that kind of pic, would you? If he didn't actually like me in *that* way then he'd have just shown me the pic when we next saw each other walking our dogs or something. Or even not ever thought about showing me Kiki in the dress. Because him thinking about wanting me to see her in the dress is sort of a sign of him liking me, isn't it?

The only bummer of the whole night is that Sam didn't say anything about meeting up. It was just the pic. But, still, that, even by itself, is pretty fantastic. And defs A Good Sign! And my party was BRILLIANT *plus* I got some fabby prezzies too. Oh yeah, apart from the one from Grace — another book token! Everyone was watching me open my presents and even though it was a bit mean when I opened the envelope I gave Grace A Look and said, 'Hellooo, are you joking?' But she was great. She didn't act upset for a second. In fact, she laughed and whispered in my ear, 'Don't forget, I'm the only one of us lot who knows your secret. I know you secretly like reading.' I love the way Grace can be sneaky and swotty at the same time. And I love it that I've got a mate who's a proper mate but that I can also tell things to without having to worry about her thinking I'm not cool. I smiled at her and then everyone said, 'What? What? What are you two on about?' But we didn't let on.

I am going to stay being the coolest, baddest girl in Year 9 — I just like reading and I like running the debating club, that's all! And, the way I see it, if you put those two together that does not equal A Major Swot.

EASTER HOLIDAYS
WEEK 2

(TUESDAY)

BEST PLACE FOR HOMEWORK

I've worked out I can do my holiday homework projects on my new laptop. (Not new-new, I know, but new to me, and it really doesn't look scuzzy and all second-hand-y, thank god, plus I put little stickers on it to 'customise' it as they say.) I'm going to ask CG if I can sit in the café sometimes when I'm not working and do my homework there. That'd be so cool – doing my homework in a hip café instead of at home like everyone else. Actually, thinking about it, if she says yes, and I'm sure she will, I'll go home, get changed, get my laptop (not ever taking it into school. As If.) and then walk back round to the café. It's only a few mins away. The café has got really popular so these days there are always a few hipsters in there and they're always on their laptops. Obvs theirs are way cooler and hipper than mine but that's okay. It's definitely going to be much easier doing homework on a laptop wherever I am. I just know it is. I hope Mum doesn't say I have to be at home doing it for some ridic reason like . . . I dunno . . . easier to concentrate at home or something else random that is so not provable.

And I forgot to tell you about when we had the first debating club. Oh man, it was totes amazeballs, legit. Mr Proper said Aly and I had to set up the room first because it was our thing. He'd organised for us to have one of the bigger classrooms and we didn't have to do much, just set out the chairs in a circle and get plastic cups and jugs from the canteen for the squash and a few plates for the biscuits. Mr Proper had got really ordinary ones – no fancy choc-chip or anything, which I suppose was to be expected. Still, free biscuits isn't bad, is it, even if they are super plain? Just before it was time to start I suddenly realised I was a bit nervous. I started panicking that no one would come, or, worse, that only major nerds would and then it would be the uncoolest thing in the world to be involved with, but I'd still have to go on doing it. But that is not what happened. You would not believe it. Loads of boys from our year came and lots of girls came too, but we kind of guessed they would, but we'd been worried that not that many boys would turn up. And guess why so many came? Because Mr Proper had made them read our project and they wanted to complain that it was, wait for it . . . sexist!

It was so brilliant. Almost every single one of the boys said that our checking who-did-what thing made the boys look they were only interested in football and hanging around in big groups and nothing else!

All the girls there were like, 'Yeah, well, that is what the majority of you are like,' and the boys answered back saying that it wasn't true and then everyone started shouting and yelling that they were right and the others were wrong. One boy, Patrick, who's not from our class (who I know is like super bright and top of everything, a bit of a boy version of Grace), said he thought Aly and I had probably 'deliberately looked to limit the boys' choices so that it would fit into our preconceived idea of what they are like', but that so wasn't true. So we said we hadn't and then everyone started disagreeing with each other. It was fantastic. We had so much fun and, best of all, in the end we managed to get some of the boys to agree with us. Patrick eventually piped up that if we promised we'd been fair then he was 'prepared to accept the project's findings'. Oooh, lucky us, eh? Still, it was good he'd said that because that meant some of the boys could then agree with him. Hah, hah, they probably reckoned agreeing with him meant it didn't look like they were actually agreeing with us, like letting us 'win', which they were in fact doing because it was our project to start with!

Mr P was really pleased with how it had gone and how
many people had turned up and 'how lively' it had all
got. I had such a good time. It was so great being part
of a huge argument. Oops, I'm supposed to say 'debate'.
It is the debating club, I guess. Also, Grace pointed
out if I always say 'arguing' instead of debating then
it looks like I only want an argument that I want to
win, instead of being 'open to debate' (her words,
natch). Obvs I've got to be okay about debating things
I don't actually agree with, basics because otherwise
Mr P might stop me doing the debating club. BTW
all the biscuits got eaten by . . . guess who . . . the
boys. They wolfed the whole lot down before any of
the girls got close to them. Typical. We should have
put that down in our project! 'If a plate of biscuits is
left out, do boys eat them all before any girls get a
chance? OR if girls get to the plate first, do they leave
some for others?' Wish I'd thought of saying that

during the club because then that would have been rock-solid proof right there and then that our project's findings were right! And the Biscuit-Scoffing Boys would not have been able to deny it! Luckily we are not doing that 'experiment' in our house because I defs eat way more biscuits than Luke. Well, according to Mum . . . But on this occasion she is probably right.

Oh yeah, just before everyone came in Aly said, 'Thanks for inviting me to the party. I had the best time.' And then she paused for a minute. For a split second I thought she might be going to say something horrible, like she used to. I don't know her that well yet so it was possible that she might, but she didn't. She carried on: 'In fact, I had the best time I've had since my mum died, so, you know, thanks.' Oh god, it was so sad I nearly burst into tears but Aly made a crazy face like she was sort of saying, 'Don't worry, I'm okay,' which was a relief.

Oh my god, you are not going to believe this. Oh man, it is major. You know that mentor-y thing where Luke 'practises' the journey to school with someone older who is already there? Yeah, well, you are never going to guess who Luke's been paired up with. Sam! Sam is at that Nerds-Only School! And they've put him with my stinky little brother! And because of Sam living round here he's going to be Luke's travel nanny or whatever they call it. Well, I think it's Sam. It must be him. Luke was blabbing on about his visit to the school with Mum and all the super boring stuff he'd done, classes they'd visited, blah, blah, blah, and the older boy who he's going to do the first few journeys with, so obvs I wasn't listening because, like, who cares, but then I heard him say 'Sam' and I thought, *Eh?* For an awful moment I thought Luke had found out something (not that there's really anything to find out, but, you know, that he's my crush or whatevs), but he hadn't – he was just talking about the guy who lives near us and is going to do the journey with him. And he's called Sam.

'What does he look like?' I asked as super caj as I could, but Luke wasn't fooled.

'Ooh, looking for a boyfriend, are you?'

'As if. And if I was I wouldn't be trying to find one at your School for Swots, that's for sure. No one fancies nerds.' (Sam might be at that school but he is not a nerd.) 'So, listen up, because that is you. You have been warned,' I replied sarkily.

'Hmm, just as well because you've got to be really bright to get into my new school and no one really bright would want you as their girlfriend, dumbo,' Luke sneered back, which really annoyed me, especially because if it is the same Sam I am worried that Luke might be right.

Maybe Sam doesn't want me as his girlfriend because he's all brainy and I'm not. I'm not saying I'm stupid, but I know I'm not exactly a brainbox, but that is mainly because I don't want to be one.

Mum got annoyed at us for bickering and suddenly shouted, 'For the love of god, will you two shut up?! I can't hear myself think!' This always makes Luke and me crack up because, as Luke has pointed out a gerzillion times, no one in the world can hear themselves think. Brains don't make a noise, so, like, derr, it is such a hilar thing to say. And, anyway, if your brain did make a noise when you were thinking it would drive you mad because your ears are so near your brain you wouldn't be able to not hear the noise it was making. And then because of us cracking up together at Mum I realised we weren't rowing any more so I quickly took the chance to ask Luke to describe this Sam guy again and it is deffo Sam. Obvs I can't be one hundred per cent but it sounds like him and he lives round here so it would be pretty amazing if there are two Sams who both live round here and both go to that school.

If it is him, I can't decide if this is a complete disaster or a good thing. When they travel together Sam might think Luke is an annoying little gnat, which he is, and then when he finds out he's my brother he might think I'm exactly the same as Luke. OR if Sam thinks Luke is great, which I admit isn't very likely, but if he does then he might think: *I must go out with Tab because she must be even greater if she's the older sister of this great guy.* Hmm, let's face it, the most likely thing is that he'll think Luke is incredibly boring, which he is, because Luke will probably bore Sam to actual death on the journey, giving him all his fascinating (not) facts about ants and planets and space shuttles, and then Sam will probably think I must be just as boring as my little brother, even though I am most defs not. The safest thing is to make sure Sam never finds out Luke is my brother – that's the best way to avoid him lumping us both together. Of course I won't need to do that if I never see Sam again. He hasn't texted since he sent the pic of Kiki in the dress, even though I texted back. I showed Gran the pic. She loved it and said she'd make more to sell through Woollies for Woofies . . . if it gets off the ground. Great, more dogs in dresses all over the place — fabulous and not at all embarrassing if people find out my gran knitted them!

EASTER HOLIDAYS WEEK 2

(SATURDAY)

WOOLLIES FOR WOOFIES GOES LIVE

So, just as I was leaving the café after work (I still get excited saying that as it is *so* amazeballs having a Saturday job and the extra money is brilliant!), CG told me that a couple of her friends wanted Gran to knit some outfits for their dogs. That is great but also completely ridic, if you ask me, but I suppose if you actually live all the time with dogs who wear knitted doggy-versions of real clothes then you're so used to it you don't think they're that amazing. But much better than that and coincidence or what, when I got home Gran said she had got, random alert, a letter from Sam's mum saying she loved Kiki's dress so much that she'd like to meet Gran to talk about starting a business selling Gran's stuff. An actual proper business. Can you believe that? And I had been so panicked that Sam's mum would think the dress was the craziest thing she'd ever seen. I know I've only met her once but she is pretty la-di-da and their house is all everything-looks-brand-new-don't-touch-anything-y. I was terrified she'd think the dress was bonkers. Which, let's face it, it actually is but not for people who are totes in love with their dogs, I guess!

I made Gran promise if this business thing works out they would defs call it Woollies for Woofies because that is a) brilliant, b) hilar and c) tells you exactly what the business is. Anyway, how amazing is that? The letter was put through the door and it didn't come via the post, so I did wonder if maybe Sam had delivered it by hand and then that made me think he deffo doesn't like me because if he did why hadn't he knocked on the door or texted me to see if I was in?

But maybe it wasn't him who delivered it. I hope not anyway. Gran is so excited about it and is going to meet Sam's mum to organise the whole thing.

Wouldn't it be amazing if it became a huge thing and celebrities starting dressing their dogs up in Gran's gear and she became a sort of designer-gear-for-dogs knitter? Oh man, that would be fantastic. Plus I'd never have to worry again about walking Basil and Scramble wearing something ridic because instead of worrying about people thinking how ridic those dogs look and, like, is-she-crazy-ish, they'd be thinking, *Wow, look at those dogs in that trendy gear*, wouldn't they? And I'd be all like super caj: 'Yeah, my gran makes all the stuff on Woollies for Woofies . . .'

A few days later, we were all hanging out and I showed everyone the photo of Kiki in the dress again and a few of Basil in different outfits, including Gran's latest one (she's knitting the whole time since she got the letter) – it is a kilt and a sort of floppy side-on hat. It's a bit like a massive deflated cushion-beret-thing called a tam-o'-shanter, according to Gran. I literally shrieked out loud when I saw him in it. 'Well, he's a Westie, he's Scottish, so he might as well have his national dress!' Gran said as she fastened his kilt and tied his hat thing on. I thought I was going to collapse it made me laugh so hard. Honestly Basil looks absolutely hilar in it. It is completely hilarious. I think it's probably the craziest outfit she's ever made. Every single one of my gang burst out laughing when they saw it. A'isha was laughing so hard she nearly weed herself. And Aly literally doubled over she was cracking up so much.

Oh yeah, Aly is one of our gang now. After my party and her telling us all about her mum and about her having to move schools loads of times it kind of made sense of why she'd gone all goth-y and grumpy. It wasn't like with Grace when we had to 'officially accept' (Grace's words, natch) her into our group. In fact, it was almost exactly the opposite – at my party Aly just said, 'So, I reckon I should be able to be in with you lot now . . .' And before anyone could say anything she went on, 'Anyway, lump or like it because there's nothing you can do to stop me.' She blurted out that last bit, I think, because she was worried we were going to tell her to go away. I don't actually know why she said it but it is a pretty out-there thing to say and so Aly! At first everyone got a bit panicky and we all looked at each other, totes confused and, TBH, a bit scared that this was her back to being stroppy, freaky Aly, so no one said a word. Then after a split second of eggy-ness Grace smiled and said, 'Remind me again where you went to charm school?' And, thank god, Aly burst out laughing and then we all did and that was that. She's one of us now.

I was telling everyone about CG's mates with dogs wanting some of Gran's stuff and about Sam's mum's letter and my amazing name for the business and then Emz had an absolutely brilliant idea. 'Why don't you suggest to your gran that they do a photo shoot of all the dogs in the different outfits and put them on a website?' 'Oh man, that would be hilar,' Aly joined in. 'I'd look at that, even though I'm never going to buy a doggy outfit!' And then A'isha (it would be her) said, 'Oh yeah, and that way you get to see Sam without having to make it obvious you're desperate to see him.' 'Hah, hah,' I replied, even though I did think that would actually be a great idea, plus a super-caj way to see him. Of course everyone immediately said they had to be at the photo shoot too.

I told Gran about the idea when I got home. 'Oh, darling, how clever of you all, that's exactly what Sam's mum and I thought. She's organising a photographer, and I'm knitting like billy-o. It's all go!' I asked Gran if my lot could all come over and help and she said yes. Gran is the best.

Just realised – it is VITAL that I make sure Luke isn't here when we do the photos because if Sam comes too (I soooo hope he does) then he'll see him and realise I am related to him – or worse that he is related to me! I really hope Sam does come with his mum. I don't suppose there's any guarantee he will. I mean, I probs wouldn't go if it was my mum doing this. Actually, that's not true, I would go because I could use it as an excuse to get to see Sam without it looking like I was super keen and desperate.

EASTER HOLIDAYS WEEK 2

(TUESDAY)

WOOLLIES FOR WOOFIES GOES MENTAL

Wow! What an amazing day! I just don't know where to start. Actually, it wasn't a complete success. There was one MAJOR disaster but I'll tell you about that later and in the end it was quite funny, I suppose, but at first it was completely awks, legit.

So we did the photo shoot with all the dogs today — a doggy fashion shoot! I have never done anything as hilar or difficult in my life. Trying to wrestle four dogs into a gerzillion different outfits, including hats and, a couple of times, booties (for the puppies obvs, even Gran wouldn't put them on a grown-up dog!), is not as easy as you'd think! Assuming, hah, hah, anyone in the history of the world apart from Gran has ever thought about how hard it would be to dress up dogs!

Sam's mum came over with their two dogs Bonnie and Kiki, but no Sam. I was so gutted but then she said (before I'd managed to super-caj ask where he was, thank god) that he was coming along later. My whole gang were there to help too, plus the photographer – the room was jam-packed. Mum had gone out in a strop, yelling at Gran that she had 'really lost her mind now'. She does not approve of this website and thinks Gran and Sam's mum are crazy for doing this whole thing. She might turn out to be right but the thing is Mum doesn't ever walk Basil and Scramble or have much to do with them ever so she doesn't actually know that loads of people are just as obsessedly in totes love with their dogs as Gran and Sam's mum and CG's mates obvs are. Mum took Luke with her, thank god, and said they'd be out all day 'away from this madhouse'. I think Mum is genuinely jealous of the attention Gran gives Basil and Scramble, which is a bit immature really. She's a grown-up and can look after herself, or she's supposed to be able to, anyway! And they are dogs; they can't exactly get their own food or pick up their own poo, YUCK, can they? BTW that is the bit of walking the dogs I REALLY HATE. Anyway, it was great that I didn't have to worry about Sam bumping into Luke and the whole game being up.

The photographer pushed all the furniture from one side of the room out of the way and then hung up a huge white plasticky sheet thing that covered one wall. Then he put a big box thing he'd brought with him right in the middle in front of the white sheet and told us that's where the dogs had to sit when he took the photos. Well, I knew straight away we were going to be in trouble! He'd obviously never met Basil or Bonnie or the puppies. 'Getting any of them to sit still is not usually an option, in my experience,' I said to the photographer, who just gave me a not very nice look.

Of course in the end it turned out I was right! We'd get each dog dressed in one of Gran's natty outfits. Every time A'isha dressed one of them she'd get the giggles and could hardly finish what she was doing. Let's face it, wrestling a puppy into a ballet dress plus tutu *is* pretty funny. The idea was that we'd get all four of them ready, take a photo of the first and then the next one would be ready to go up onto the box while we changed the one who'd just had his/her photo taken. Yeah, well, good idea, but as soon as we got Basil (he was first) up on the box, he jumped straight off and obvs loved that so much he then started jumping up and down off the box. You should have seen the look on the photographer's face – not a happy bunny. 'Right, we'll let Basil calm down and put Bonnie up on the box,' Gran said, trying to take control. I could tell she was a bit embarrassed about how naughty Basil was being, especially in front of Sam's mum, who, TBH, did have a face on her like she couldn't believe what was going on. Hah, that is, of course, before it was Bonnie's turn! Because Bonnie was as badly behaved as Basil. We put her up on the box and for a split second she looked like she was going to be brilliant and just sit (and show Basil up) but she didn't – she stood up and did a sort of

massive leap off the box, kind of using it as a spring-
board over to the other side of the room. As soon
as she landed she looked round at Basil as if she was
saying, 'What do you think of that?!' Emz cracked
up immediately. And then Aly did too. So then the
rest of us did, except the adults. They obviously did
not think us all laughing was helping the situation.

Next we tried the puppies in matching romper suits
and bonnets (not kidding). Blue for Scramble and
pink for Kiki (a bit sexist, I thought, but Gran said
that's what would sell). They actually managed to stay
still and the photographer got a few shots but then,
yes, you guessed it, Scramble weed himself! 'Oh for
goodness' sake,' Sam's mum cried out and at that
exact moment Kiki weed herself too. It was so funny.
None of us lot could stop laughing. It was hilar and
the more annoyed the grown-ups got the funnier it
was. You know that thing when you know you've got
to stop laughing because grown-ups are getting all
het up and it just makes you laugh more? Well, that
was us!

Eventually after Gran and Sam's mum had changed
the puppies and cleared up the mess with the

photographer looking on as if he'd never seen anything like it in his life, we came up with a plan. We put each dog up on the box and then, either side of the box one of us (it was me and Grace to start with) would lie on the floor pressing sticks into the side of whichever dog was up there to hold them in place. This was the photographer's genius idea and, amazingly, for a tiny bit it did work, but then Scramble (it would be him) thought the sticks were for him to chase, so he started doing that thing he does of whizzing round and round in a circle, trying to nip the sticks on either side of him. Well, that was it, my whole gang just burst out laughing and then all four dogs suddenly seemed to think it was the most hilar thing too so they all started dancing and prancing about, jumping up and down off furniture, including the box, and barking and yelping – it was like they were having a dog rave!

Well, the photographer completely lost it. He packed up his stuff and walked out, saying he'd never met such unprofessional dogs in his life! *Hellooo*, I thought, *professional dogs?* No one had ever said these dogs were models or anything. Ridic. But then I saw Sam's mum's face and I was really worried she was going to walk out too and then the whole Woollies for Woofies wouldn't happen and Gran would be upset, and, plus, selfish I know, but then maybe Sam would go off me. And then Grace had a brainwave. Brilliant, swotty, always-knows-what-to-do Grace suddenly piped up: 'Instead of putting up photos of the dogs in their various outfits on the website why don't we just film them mucking about like they are now, in all their different gear? It'd be much more fun and people would still see the stuff.' I saw Gran and Sam's mum look at each other, like they were both thinking it was a great idea and Grace seized her chance. 'I'll film them on my phone. I'm pretty good with it and it's good quality and I'll upload it for you too.' Oh man, just when I thought the whole thing was going to go belly up Grace saved the day. So that's what we did and it was perfect. Grace shot loads of film on her phone of the dogs in their various outfits all mucking about with each other really sweetly. It looked really natural and not posey, as well as funny. We were all really pleased, including Sam's mum, but then disaster . . .

We were just packing up, putting away all the outfits and stuff and the doorbell rang and it was Sam! I was so pleased. He came in and everyone was, thank god, all caj and not, 'Oh you've come, that's so great because Tab's been waiting for you all day long.' I know no one, except maybe A'isha, would actually say something like that out loud, but I was worried for a minute that they might act like that's what they were thinking. Sam sat on the floor and started playing with Kiki and Scramble, who were jumping all over him, and Sam's mum started to tell him about how the photo shoot had gone wrong and Gran made tea and got biscuits out for everyone and I was thinking, *It's so caj and relaxed and not at all pressure-y Sam being here.* And then . . . aaargh . . . Luke walked in. No Mum, just Luke. I hadn't heard the front door so there was no warning, suddenly there he was, my annoying, moronic, mankenstein brother standing there, looking super surprised and staring at us all like we were stark naked or something.

Sam, still sitting on the floor, covered in puppies and looking confused said, 'Luke? What are you doing here?' Luke laughed and said, 'I was going to ask you exactly the same thing. I live here.'

I, like a crazy loon, jumped into the space between Sam and Luke and cried out, 'No, he doesn't!'

Sam gave me a weird look, while Luke said, 'What are you talking about?!'

I don't know what craziness got hold of me except that I was so desperate that Sam wouldn't find out he was my brother that I sort of lost my head. Then I mouthed silently at Sam, 'He's mad,' but Sam didn't seem to get it. And then Luke leant round me, looking at Sam, and said, 'Anyway, what are *you* doing here?' And then I, like a complete moron, tried to block him with my body, swaying from side to side as Luke tried to get round me, and whispered to Sam, 'Ignore him, he's the boy from next door. He's nuts.' Sam nodded at me like he understood, stood up and said to Luke, 'Okay, shall we nip round to your house, mate?' Luke pushed me out of the way. 'We're *in my house.* I don't know what she's up to but I live here, this halfwit is my sister and that's our gran,' he said, pointing at Gran.

I don't know why or how but I just sort of yelled, 'Nooooo, that is not true!' The whole room looked at me then – Emz, A'isha, Grace, Aly, Gran, Sam and his mum, every one of them wearing the same expression that basics said, 'What the hell are you playing at?!'

After what felt like the longest, eggiest silence of my life the penny dropped for Luke, 'Aah, I know what's going on. Tab fancies you,' he said, nodding at Sam, 'and she thinks you won't fancy her back if you find out I'm her brother. I wondered why she was so interested in the Sam from my new school. She must have guessed it was you!' And then he turned to me and laughed. 'BUSTED!'

I wanted the ground to open up and swallow me. I have never ever been so embarrassed in my life. And, to make it all worse, as if it could get any worse, everyone suddenly started moving around, busying themselves with random stuff they so obviously didn't need to do to cover up how embarrassed they were too and how they didn't know what to say. Pretty soon my lot all sort of slunk off together and Luke went off and made himself a sandwich like nothing had happened and he didn't know what the big deal was. Sam's mum and Gran started a loud conversation about nothing at all and I just stood there and stared at the floor, desperately trying not to cry with shame. And then, thank god, Scramble came up to me and started playing around my legs, so I bent down to pick him up and as I stood back up I caught sight of Sam. He was giving me what I thought was a look saying 'You are the most pathetic thing in the world'. Obvs I immediately looked away. I just knew I'd never

ever be able to look him in the eye ever again. Then I heard him say: 'Shall we take the dogs for a walk?' Oh man, I wanted to die of gratitude, but I was still too embarrassed to speak in case it gave someone a chance to ask me what on earth I'd been doing pretending I didn't know Luke, so I nodded quickly.

'That was pretty random, Tab,' Sam said after we'd walked for a bit in total silence, and for that whole time I'd been in a complete panic, thinking, *He's going to really tell me off, plus tell me he doesn't like me in 'that' way.* 'Yeah, erm, sorry. I don't really know what I was doing,' I replied, and tried to laugh. I'm pretty sure my laugh sounded totes phoney, basics because it was, and even though he'd suggested we take the dogs out I was still nowhere near over the trauma of what a total idiot I'd made of myself. 'Well,' Sam said, 'I've never had a brother or sister to be ashamed of but if I had one and he was like Luke I can see why you'd never ever want anyone to know you were related to him.' For a minute I thought I'd heard him wrong but I hadn't. I couldn't believe he was being so horrible about my little brother. *He hardly even knows him*, I was thinking, while I was boiling up inside. And then I just let rip. 'He's all right and he's super bright and is sometimes quite funny. He's only eleven. You don't even know what you're talking about!' I was about to walk off when I saw Sam break into a huge smile. 'See? You do like him really.' And then I realised he'd only been horrid about him to make me defend him. I laughed out loud and then said, 'Maybe, but not that much,' and Sam starting laughing. And then . . . oh my god, you will not believe this, I don't know how it happened or where it came from or who started but we . . . kissed! Sam and I kissed on the lips!

It was a proper super dreamy actual kiss. We didn't do tongues, YUCK, but it was defs a romantic kiss. It was absolutely lovely. I can't actually believe it. And then out of the corner of my eye – I know you're supposed to close your eyes when you kiss someone up close, or at least I think you are, and Sam did have his eyes closed, but I sneaked one of mine open, which was just as well because I caught Bonnie doing a poo right in the middle of the pavement. Unfortunately it made me snigger because here I was kissing my dream boy and his dog was choosing that exact moment to do a poo – it was so random and in a way so typical of my luck. That made Sam open his eyes and say, 'What?!' I think he was worried that I was laughing at how he kissed. As if. But I just smiled and said, 'Need a poo bag?' and nodded towards where Bonnie was doing her thing. Sam turned round and said, 'Great, nice timing, Bonnie,' and then we both laughed. IT WAS AMAZEBALLS. BRILLIANT AND COMPLETELY FANTASTIC IN EVERY POSSIBLE WAY. (Not Bonnie pooing, obvs!)

But, if you think about it, it is pretty hilar that my first ever kiss should happen at the exact same moment my gran's dog's girlfriend, or whatever Bonnie is, has a poo! Not exactly the most romantic story ever, is it? But it is very funny I think and is going to make my gang completely crack up. Who cares if it's not all fairy-tale, girly-girly. We did kiss, and it was fab and a dog did a poo at the same time! Like they say — shit happens! Hah, hah!

EASTER HOLIDAYS WEEK 3

(MONDAY)

MUM DROPS A BOMBSHELL

God, today has probably been the weirdest day of my life. So, I got home and obvs I was in a brilliant mood, so even when Luke at supper was trying his absolute hardest to wind me up about Sam he didn't manage to get a rise out of me. I was like 'Yeah, whatevs' to every single thing he said. And then, sort of out of nowhere, Mum said, 'I need to tell you both something,' in such a weird, calm voice we both stopped bickering straight away. I looked at her and had a horrible moment when I thought she was going to say she was ill or something terrible. But that wasn't it. 'I've talked to Gran and she's okay with this . . .' Luke and I looked at each other, both thinking the same thing: *Okay with what?!* Mum suddenly looked all teary and I started to get really worried. 'What is it, Mum? Spit it out!' I shouted at her. I wasn't trying to be horrid but she was really freaking me out. 'Frank and I have been seeing each other for six months and we've decided to celebrate by going on a long trip around the world together.' I was so relieved and couldn't believe she'd made such a big heavy deal with this announcement. And then she said, 'For three months,' and looked at Luke and then me, giving us both a sort of mix between an 'I'm sorry' and 'Is that okay?' face. At first I was so incredibly relieved it wasn't proper awful news I thought, *Yeah, fine, whatevs, who cares?* I just said, 'It's fine, don't get all het up, it's not like you're leaving us on our own, is it?' But Luke looked a bit upset. 'Will you be back in time for me starting my new school?' he asked Mum. I could tell he was trying not to cry. 'Of course I will!' Mum replied. 'And I'll Skype whenever I can and send you emails,' she continued. 'Yeah, and buy us lots of presents,' I said, trying to make everything not so heavy and dramatic. I mean, it is pretty major, I admit, but it is not the-end-of-the-world major.

Except that now that I'm thinking about it I have to admit it is quite a big thing, isn't it? Not seeing your kids for three whole months? It didn't really help that all of my mates (I Instagrammed everyone in a group thing) thought it was not actually that brilliant of my mum, which, I guess it isn't. But, you know, three months isn't that bad, is it? If she was going to prison for some murder or something really major she'd be away for much longer. I did think one thing, though, when she came in to say goodnight and check I was okay. I said, 'BTW no coming back married to him, all right?' Mum laughed and said, 'It's a deal,' but then as she was closing the door I said, 'Promise,' and she did. But you never know with parents' promises, do you? She had better not marry him, that is for sure.

Bleurgh. I am not having HIM as a stepdad with that beard, even if he is brilliant at making mocktails.

Just as I was about to go to sleep Luke knocked on my door. I knew he must be feeling wobbly because usually he never knocks. 'Do you feel funny about Mum's news?' he said, inching in to my room. I jumped up and pulled him down onto the carpet so we were both sitting up against the side of my bed. 'Actually, stinky little bro, I've just been thinking about all the amazing things we'll get to do without Mum around to stop us! You know Gran is much cooler about stuff than Mum ever is. And, anyway, she'll be back before you know it and while she's away you can turn her room into a dungeon or whatever you like.' Luke got really excited about that and finally went back to his room all cheered up about the crazy nerdy things he was going to build in her room. It was funny because although I do feel weird about this I also feel quite excited. And it feels soooo grown up too. And I am right, Gran is so going to let us do much more than Mum usually does.

So, only a tiny bit into being fourteen years old, I have got a job, tick, done something I like at school without turning into a swot, tick, had the best party ever, tick, got a boyfriend, tick, and become an orphan, tick. TBH, pretty amazeballs, legit.

Yeah, yeah, I know I'm not an actual in-real-life orphan but that sounds way better and cooler and more interesting than the facts, doesn't it?

Oh yeah, and I can say I've got a boyfriend because Sam is officially (as Grace would say) my boyf. I know because he texted me 'night, night' and no one would text that to someone they'd just kissed if they didn't want them to be their actual girlfriend, would they? I can't wait to tell my gang about the kiss . . . (And the poo, natch!)

Thank you for choosing a Piccadilly Press book.

If you would like to know more about our authors, our books or if you'd just like to know what we're up to, you can find us online.

www.piccadillypress.co.uk

You can also find us on:

We hope to see you soon!